The Rise of Black Sky

Oghosasere, "Samuel"
Uwensuyi-Edosomwan

The Writers Game

The Rise of Black Sky

Oghosasere, "Samuel" Uwensuyi-Edosomwan

The Writers Game

Disclaimer

The Writers Game

8936 Northpointe Executive Park Drive, Ste 260,

Huntersville, NC 28078

info@thewritersgame.com

THE RISE OF BLACK SKY

www.thewritersgame.com

ISBN: 979-8-9877109-2-0

eBook ISBN: 979-8-9877109-3-7

Printed in The United States of America

Contents

In the world of words, where imagination soars and dreams take shape, it is with immense gratitude that I dedicate this book, "Rise of Black Sky," to the U-Edosomwan Family. Your nurturing hearts have taught me the power of perseverance and the importance of embracing one's dreams. With your constant presence as guiding stars, I have embarked on this literary adventure, knowing that I have an unwavering support system that believes in the power of storytelling.

To Danielle Gusby, this dedication holds a special place in my heart. Your unwavering support, encouragement, and belief in the depths of my imagination have propelled me to conquer uncharted realms within the pages of "Rise of Black Sky." Your faith in my abilities has given me the strength to transform mere words into a captivating tapestry of emotions and adventures.

The Great Pain

Danny was a young man who was the most talented cultivator in his hometown. Being able to awaken a battle-oriented spiritual manifestation in the wastelands was impressive since the odds of doing that in the wastelands were slim without special resources tailored to him or his bloodline. But he loved his family and wanted a safer and better life away from their cold, poverty-stricken hometown. He, like so many people just like him, went to the City of Noel's annual recruitment event.

Out of almost fifty participants, he made it to the top ten, and with that, his life was going to be set. He brought his whole family with him, which included his father, mother, grandmother, older brother, and two younger into the city with him. The first time he stepped through the gates, he felt the difference.

With a permanent environment formation, the snowy ground under his feet turned from cold to lukewarm. Danny could no longer see his own breath in the air. From there, he was taken to one of the small homes closest to the gate and told that he would need to quickly increase his cultivation level if he wanted a better home that had more space. For almost six months, he learned the basics of his guard duties and got to the peak of mid-level tier-one, which let him move his family further from the gate to have more protection. For the first time in his life, Danny forgot the feeling of hunger. He also had a mentor who taught him the ways of the spear, resources to use as he pleased, and the security of being under someone no one wanted to mess with, which filled him with confidence.

One day before the season of Evil Frost was upon them, Danny was doing his usual guard duties under his mentor when he saw *it*. A damaged, worn-out cart, seen from a distance, was coming toward them. When it finally arrived, Danny saw the Immortal Slave that he had only heard a single whisper about and was unconsciously jealous of because of his good looks. But after hearing his mentor remind him of his future as a slave, Danny calmed down.

The next day, all hell broke loose. A giant Deep Snow clan warrior had charged into the city by himself and singlehandedly battled against one hundred people with nothing but his body. No one in the outer layer of the city could leave a mark or harm him. Each person, including Danny, was dealt with.

They received a strike to the gut or a broken limb. The fearful ones simply surrendered and ran away.

Danny was lying on the ground, having woken up from being unconscious for less than an hour and feeling like he couldn't catch his breath. As he lay down looking at the sky, he saw an eye-catching dark dot appear in the sky. At first, it was too small to notice the dot without the light it absorbed around it, but the mysterious object kept growing until it was the size of a tall-story building. As it grew in size, the more powerful the dot became. Eventually, Danny noticed that his tier-one armor started to lose its protective features. It was as if it was restricting something.

Suddenly, Danny noticed he was floating off the ground a few inches. Looking around, he saw that anything without tier-one energy was floating into the sky toward the huge dark circle: food, materials, furniture, and people. Danny watched as family members of the guards floated into the sky. They all screamed in terror as the pull of the dark circle continued.

Danny felt his armor getting weaker, so he started channeling his own source energy. The pull finally lost its effect, and he was on the ground. Danny started running toward his home but only found his father and older brother at the house. The women had gone to the market and had been caught up in the huge attack.

For weeks, the city was shut down. All that was left of the people in the outer layer were the guards, who wore their armor, and the civilians, who stayed in their homes. Danny's whole family was devastated. All his father could do was drink his pain away and focus only on cultivating. He wanted to be able to join the city guards when they got revenge for their loved ones.

Danny's older brother had been helping him deal with his grief when, one day, all the tier-two warriors entered the outer layer and started mercilessly branding everyone who was tier-one. While the tier-one people outnumbered the tier-two warriors by ten to one, the former group was not in the same league. Danny was with his family when his mentor entered their home with a branding tool and held them down with his superior speed and strength. He quickly branded each of them. When the brand hit, Danny felt as if his bloodline was disappearing, and he gave into sadness to weep for his new fate. His father, however, roared like a mad beast who was losing all hope of being able to avenge his beloved mother, wife, and daughters. He jumped at Danny's mentor, hoping to die. Unfortunately, all he received was a strike to his gut from the bottom of a spear.

Danny's mentor told them to get out of the home and make their way to the new slave quarters. Although weak from the branding, Danny felt like he still had his speed and strength.

But he would never again be able to manifest his spear, and because of that, he had no chance of resisting his fate. While Danny tried to pull his father together, he noticed both his mentor and older brother had disappeared. Walking outside with his father, Danny saw his brother sprinting toward the gate. He noticed there were many others doing the same. Danny couldn't figure out why they were all doing this until he saw none of them stopping. They just continued into the blizzard.

Danny never saw his brother again. The survivors of the branding could do nothing but weep as they left their homes and went to the new slave quarters. The battle that took the lives of so many people that day who were sucked into the dark circle would become known as the Great Pain. All those who survived would pass on the story to anyone who would listen.

Chapter One

Clearing of The Fog

S ince the beginning of life, there have always been many undeniable truths. One of the most important truths is that the powerful rule over the masses like kings, while the weak lower their heads in fear and shame. Like gravity, this is a fundamental part of reality that can't simply be changed, no matter how much you beg or curse against fate. An unlimited number of people from the past, present, and future try to fight their lot in life only to end up being crushed by the very fate they despise.

In the universe known as The Cloud Domain, there is a planet similar to Earth called Origin. Earth and Origin share many things in common, but other things are so different that no one in their right mind would claim that both planets are the same. The most significant difference is that, throughout the multiverse, there is an energy that flows through the environment that has caused many people, animals, and even objects to acquire different types of energy such as life force energy, magic, and even cosmic energy. That energy is known as source energy.

The source is the beginning of all roots of power throughout the multiverse and is limitless in its potential. For those who have it, depending on their level of control, it is possible to quickly flatten a city or even eradicate a mountain range or two. That is why those unlucky enough to be born without the ability to generate this energy aren't even seen as living beings by the average source user. A life of servitude and discrimination awaits them, for without power, who can they stand against?

Most have accepted this as a fact and can only live each day hoping that a powerful source user doesn't wipe them off the face of the planet. However, there are those whose spirits can't be broken no matter their situation.

Early one winter morning, before the sun was even up, there stood two guards with spears in their hands at the northern entrance of the City of Noel, a small city in the middle of nowhere with technology the level of medieval times.

While training his rookie guard, a senior officer saw something growing larger in the distance. Pushing a large wagon that was hauling supplies and wearing barely any clothes to keep the cold out of their bodies, four of the five slaves struggled to keep the wagon moving while the overseer, Rod, rode in the back.

The rookie guard asked his superior, "Who are they?"

In a smug tone, his superior replied, "Those things can't be referred to as people. Those are the property of The Merchant. I know why you don't know. That wagon is gone for six months each year, so it must have just returned."

"Where do they go?" asked the rookie.

"They go into the wasteland to collect valuable resources, which are then auctioned off at the annual Grand Auction."

The rookie asked, "Why would The Merchant send normal, powerless people into the wasteland when hiring source users who are more likely to succeed would be simpler?"

"Because The Merchant genuinely doesn't care if those things live or die. Well . . . except for *one* of those things. The Merchant doesn't pay anything for each trip except the overseer's fee. So, whenever they bring back something valuable, he makes money with a low investment and usually a high reward," the senior officer said.

After the wagon made a full stop at the entrance, the senior guard called out to the overseer, "Rod, how was the journey?"

Rod replied, "You know, found lots of valuables. Lost three-quarters of these worthless things and three wagons to multiple packs of tier-two upper-level wolves."

The senior officer started to laugh, "Haha! So, same as always."

The rookie guard spoke up in a terrified voice, "Who or what the hell is that?"

The senior officer turned his head to look at his subordinate pointing at a mountain of a man—the only thing in bondage showing no sign of fatigue. His shoulders were as broad as a valley, and he towered over the other things like a skyscraper. The most surprising feature about this mysterious thing was his pale, flawless white skin. If he lay down in the snow, it would be impossible to find him. Not even the city's richest woman of nobility could match this creature's beauty. His eyes were a piercing blue that was as deep as the ocean and gave off waves of power.

The senior officer spat on the ground, clearly annoyed at the thought that a slave was more handsome than him. "That is what some people in the city call the Immortal Slave. No matter how difficult the task, this thing will complete it."

The rookie asked, "If he is so formidable, why would he be trapped in a situation like this? I'm a low-tier level one, but even I know I wouldn't be able to even touch this guy without losing many body parts."

"I don't know, and I really don't care as long as it doesn't cause problems for me. Why would I look into the situation of a mere slave?" Even while saying this, the envy in the senior officer's voice was so thick that someone would have to be blind, deaf, and dumb not to pick up on it.

"Makes sense," said the rookie, showing more arrogance in his tone and eyes.

Meanwhile, the slaves started to push the wagon again. The weakest of them slipped on the snow-covered ground. Struggling to get back up, with only one arm remaining on his body and one eye in his head, the slave trembled from the cold. Infuriated that they had stopped again, the overseer created a whip out of the fire and unleashed a barrage of hits all over the slave's body.

"Useless bastard thing! How dare you waste my precious time! My son is turning seventeen today, and I won't miss another moment with my pride and joy."

Each hit left another deep scar on the body of the feeble slave, but he didn't let out a single sound from his mouth. His eyes were lifeless and dull, as if the whipping was happening to someone else.

The next moment, the Immortal Slave climbed on top of the weakest slave, protecting him from the overseer's whips. While the whips left scars on the weakest slave, they bounced off the flesh of the Immortal Slave. The overseer stopped and barked at them after a few hits land on the Immortal Slave.

"For twelve years, I have been dealing with you two: the so-called Immortal Slave and his only weakness". The overseer curled up his whip in anger and said, "If both of you want to live to see another day, then that senseless fool needs to do what it is told to do."

Even while releasing his fire whip, others could tell how angry the overseer was that his technique had no effect, once again, on the Immortal Slave. Standing back up, the Immortal Slave helped the weakest slave back to his feet. Side by side, they began to push the wagon once again and slowly faded into the darkness, heading toward the largest mansion in the city.

Two hours after the wagon incident, the Immortal Slave and the weakest slave were back at their shack in a slave town—a dirty, broken-down part of town that was so disgusting that even the rats avoided the area. The Immortal Slave helped his friend to the two mats stacked on top of each other in the shack after quickly removing the dust and spider webs. Laying down his friend, the Immortal Slave began to apply an herbal salve to help heal the fresh wounds. After that, he began to bandage his friend's wounds.

"Wow, I can't believe it's been twelve years since we first came here. So much has changed, and yet things are still the same," said the Immortal Slave. While talking mostly to himself, he wrapped the bandage around his friend's legs.

He continued, "You and I were the youngest ones back then. No one said we would survive for long. I would cry myself to sleep every night thinking about my family and the kingdom we lost because I was the weakest. I would never reach my quota, and most days, I was supposed to starve. But you were there for me, giving me most of your food and even taking the blame for my mistakes."

"Even though you can't talk, your facial expressions have never changed. Everyone said you were a mindless fool, but I never cared what any of them said because I saw something amazing the first time you stood up for me. You have been an unwavering spirit that is willing to help others in need."

"Rod the overseer tried to kill me when I beat his son four years ago that one time when he came to abuse us with his horrible friends, but you got in the middle of us. No matter how much he whipped, burned, pummeled, or cut you, you were an unbendable wall that wouldn't yield to anything or anyone."

"That was the moment I knew what strength was, and thanks to you, I was able to train my body to take physical pain. Those weird mantras I heard you say all those years ago helped me forge my body into a weapon. Whenever I trained while reciting those words, I felt my body fill up with raw energy. Because of that, I'm so close to having a break-through. Right now, I have been holding back on increasing my body's power because if anyone realized that I'm much stronger than just a level two mid-peak source user, there is no way that they would keep me alive. But the time has finally come. After many years of training, observing, and planning, we can finally do what no one else has even dared to dream of. We can finally escape with as many of our brethren as possible. Every year, the overseer has a big birthday party for his son, causing the day we return to always be the least secure. Most guards will be drinking and having too much fun to be prepared for me. Once I break through, my body will be as strong as a peak level two source user, and I'll be able to distract the attention of the whole city. While the guards are trying to stop me, you and everyone else can get outside the city to meet at the settlement we created in the wasteland. Finally, our nightmare will be over, and we can create new lives. I'll ask my Min to watch over you and lead everyone to safety."

After talking to his friend, who had never responded to him since the day they met twelve years prior, the Immortal Slave sat down and watched the weak slave slowly close his eye and go to sleep. Looking over his best friend's abused and damaged body, the Immortal Slave could not help but remember the horrible torture his friend had endured. Before the Immortal Slave gained his strength and began protecting his friend, the poor soul lost his left eye and right arm. But that was only the visible damage.

The Immortal Slave could do nothing but burn with rage whenever he thought of the day two years ago when he returned to the shack to find his friend had had his genitals mutilated. To this day, the culprit had never been found. Still, it was the biggest regret the Immortal Slave held in his heart.

One hour later, Min walked into the shack. She was a beautiful girl with green eyes like emeralds and long, silky black hair that reached her slim waist. She, too, was enslaved, but she worked inside The Merchant's home. She was similar to the Immortal Slave in that she lost her home and family after they were defeated by an enemy kingdom. Even while wearing rags, Min still had the grace of a lady among the nobility. Though she was beautiful, the thing that attracted the Immortal Slave to her the most was the kind smile she always kept on her face. Because of that smile, he felt like he could overcome anything.

After quickly kissing and embracing Min, the Immortal Slave went over his plan with her and continued plotting. "Now that everything is ready, I can finally give you the map to the settlement in the wasteland. This has all the safest routes. Soon, we can finally get married and become one. I'm sorry that I cannot give myself to you while still in bondage, but my virginity means so much to me and my ancestors. Soon, I'll be able to propose as a free man."

Min looked him directly in his eyes and said, "Nothing would make me happier than to live the rest of my life with you, whether as a slave or free. I just want to be with you."

The Immortal Slave could barely hold back his tears. "I don't deserve someone as amazing as you, but I promise that as long as I love you, the only way harm will come to you is after the enemy steps over my body."

"Everything is going to change today. I can feel it," said Min. She flashed a smile so bright that the Immortal Slave felt like it was the first time he had really seen her smile, which made him happy but also left him with an uneasy feeling he couldn't explain. It was like her smile had a deeper meaning. "I have to leave before anyone notices that I'm gone from The Merchant's house. I'll be back here when the time comes to start the plan." She walked out the front door into the early morning.

After seeing her go, the Immortal Slave meditated on one side of the shack. "To be fully prepared, I must rest my mind and body. I must be ready for anything." He entered a deep state of meditation. His consciousness sank into his body, and he moved source energy within his bones, muscles, and organs to strengthen them.

A few minutes after he had entered his deep trance, someone in the shack began to move. With brown skin and countless marks scarring almost ninety percent of his body, the weakest slave, also known as the Immortal Slave's best friend, slowly got up from his mat and quietly stepped to one of the two windows. Looking outside, the dull, lifeless look in his eyes was gone. It was as if it had never been there. Instead, it was replaced with a glare so full of hate that it looked like he abhorred the very world itself. Words like "hate" and "rage" were too mild to describe the emotions contained inside the weakest slave. Even the words he spoke to himself carried a weight of anger so suffocating and overbearing that one would believe he could change the room's temperature with his presence alone.

"Everything is almost in place. It's about time to end this," said the weakest slave, also known as Weakness. Somehow, without making a sound, he jumped out the window and moved silently toward the overseer's home.

Chapter Two

The Plan Begins

O nly one word could describe the pitiful scene at the banquet hall for the overseer's son's celebration. With almost a hundred guards sprawled out on the ground with blood splashed onto the snow, either due to broken bones or them being unconscious, you would think that there would be lots of noise. However, the area was dead silent, except for the sound of heavy breathing and evil laughter. Destruction was everywhere—from the caved-in giant gate on the ground to the destroyed furniture and overturned tables. Even the walls had large holes everywhere. But who could be able to bring such devastation to a tier-two city? Who else but he Immortal Slave.

Bound by chains and breathing heavily, the Immortal Slave knelt on both knees in the snow with a gaping wound bleeding out profusely on the left side of his abdomen. While in pain, he wasn't even slightly concerned about his injury. He could only look ahead at the two people in front of him and ask, "Why? Why would you, of all people, betray me?"

The Immortal Slave finished his meditation and checked out his body's condition. By simply punching, he was able to generate a force that was powerful enough to collapse a non- tier small building. As long as the building didn't have any source energy, he could easily destroy it. Once he was done with testing his physical condition and strength, he felt more confident in himself and his plan. He sat down in his meditation spot and looked at Weakness, who was sitting up on top of the two mats after waking up with his usual dull, lifeless look in his eye.

After being together for so long, the Immortal Slave was used to the endless silence between the two of them and used all the time he had left to consolidate his strength and eat as much of the weekly ration as possible so that he would be ready for the journey back to the wasteland. When the appointed time came, Min arrived at the door. They quickly went over the plan once again to minimize as many mistakes as possible. They discussed everything from the amount of time they would have to move between checkpoints before the guards made their rounds to how much damage the Immortal Slave had to cause to draw enough guards away from other parts of the city. They agreed on how long the Immortal Slave would have to fight to keep the attention on himself and gain enough time for the slaves to get far away from the city so that they wouldn't get caught. The last thing they went over was how many rations each person would need to bring for the trip to make it to their settlement.

With everything in order, the Immortal Slave got up and walked to the door. He put his right hand on the shack one last time, remembering everything that had happened over the last twelve years, and felt his resolve strengthen even more. He turned to Min and Weakness and said, "I'll see you guys later."

Min looked up at him with moist eyes and said, "I believe in you."

With those final words, the Immortal Slave put on his disguise made of tier-one upper-level wolf skin and made his way outside the city walls near the southern gate in the opposite direction of the wasteland.

With half an hour to spare, the Immortal Slave checked his disguise to ensure that it looked close enough to what he intended to trick the guards that he was a part of the Deep Snow clan. He made sure his mask would hold when he started moving at high speeds.

With everything in order, he sat down and started meditating in the bushes. This was a practice the Immortal Slave used to rid himself of most of his worries. Because he had a major problem for so many years, he struggled to fall asleep. Due to some deep trauma he'd experienced as a child, he hadn't been able to sleep for almost five years. It was around that time that he heard the mantra come from Weakness's mouth. At first, he didn't know what it was, but after he recited the full chant in his mind, the massive fatigue disappeared. It felt like he had completed the chant within seconds. However, it took four hours. From then on, the Immortal Slave never slept because he could use the mantra to rest his body and mind. Over time, his body grew stronger and stronger.

Finally, the chime of the hourly bell rang out, and he knew it was time to act. Standing up from his position, the Immortal Slave slowly walked toward the southern gate. Four guards were stationed at the gate: two at the top and two at the front entrance. Barely focused and just letting their minds wander, one of the guards on top saw something come out of the forest line and started straining his eyes to make it out. Covered in white wolf fur, he saw a giant of a man approach them. As soon as he realized what it was, he began to panic.

"It's the Deep Snow clan. They are attacking again. Sound the alarm. Everyone knows when you see one of them, then ten are hiding in wait to attack!"

Once the alarm was sounded, sixteen level one mid-tier guards hurried to the gate.

Once the Immortal Slave saw more guards at the gate, he began to pick up speed from a slow walk to a light jog, but he was still some distance from the gate.

The guards were more focused on finding the other Deep Snow warriors than on the single warrior that was in front of them, the most senior-level guard ordered two close- range fighter guards to attack the lone enemy. The two began sprinting toward the Immortal Slave and manifested their source spirit weapons. Being mid-tier level one source spirit users, they moved as fast as professional athletes within a short amount of time. Almost within reach of the Immortal Slave, one guard swung his source spear at the target's head while the other stabbed their source knife directly into the Immortal Slave's heart.

Thinking the enemy was finished, the senior guard near the gate focused his full attention on finding the other Deep Snow warriors. As he turned away from the lone enemy, he heard the screams of two distinct voices. Completely surprised, he looked back and saw both of his men on the ground with at least one of their limbs broken. The most surprising part was that the enemy had dealt with both of them so quickly.

Once the Immortal Slave passed the two guards, he increased his speed and moved at the same speed as the previous enemies. Startled, the senior guard hastily ordered the long-range unit to target him. Ten men manifested their source spirit weapons: crossbows, bows and arrows, spears, and a hand cannon. They took aim. The bow and spear users were the first to fire. The projectiles moved quickly through the air and, within seconds, were trailing the enemy. At the very last moment, the Immortal Slave sidestepped the attacks and continued forward.

Next, the crossbow users loaded their source bolts. The senior guard ordered them not to shoot their shots at the same time, but instead, half shot first and the other half shot where the Immortal Slave dodged. The first half let their bolts fly, and just as before, the enemy sidestepped the projectiles. But in the middle of his dodge, the Immortal Slave noticed the second volley. Instead of just trying to dodge, the Immortal Slave crossed his arms in front of his face and tanked the hits. Expecting the bolts to pierce through the creature, the senior guard was startled by the sight of them bouncing off the enemy's skin.

Finally losing his cool, the senior guard placed all his hopes on their trump card: the hand cannon user. He was the only one of the guards with tier-two power, so the most senior guard had confidence in his subordinate's ability to blow up Deep Snow clan members because his kill count was in the hundreds. Filling the hand cannon and its ammo with all his fire source spirit energy, the guard shot off a bomb so powerful that it could blow away a small house. The bomb headed for the area right in front of the enemy.

When the Immortal Slave saw the glowing bomb, he didn't stop or try to dodge it.

Instead, he jumped into the air and caught it with one hand. At that point, the guards panicked frantically, and the most senior guard screamed for everyone to scatter. As soon as the guards were far enough away from the gate, the Immortal Slave threw the bomb directly at the gate and watched as the level two gate caved inward from the heat and force of the explosion.

With many guards scattered in the snow, bruised and beaten, the Immortal Slave stepped into the city and screamed the word "destroy" from the top of his lungs in the language of the Deep Snow clan. After hearing that scream, more guards began pouring in the direction of the southern gate.

As he was being surrounded, the Immortal Slave thought to himself, *This isn't enough guards to leave the northern gate unprotected enough for Min to take care of them on her own. I have to go with the worst-case plan and head for the overseer's son's birthday celebration.*

Stretching his body and loosening his muscles, he looked at the guards, who seemed scared of the monster before their eyes. He got into a crouching position and said "come" in the Deep Snow clan's language. At that one word, every guard in the area rushed toward the Immortal Slave, and the massive battle began.

Chapter Three

The Beautiful Lies

One hour after the attack began, the Immortal Slave stood at one of the gates that led deeper into the city. The City of Noel is structured in a way that the closer anyone got to the center, the stronger the walls, gates, and guards were. The gate in front of the Immortal Slave was so powerful that no force below peak level two could cause any damage to it. This was the main reason why the Immortal Slave trained so hard to be able to destroy it one day.

The Immortal Slave took a stance right in front of the gate. He closed his eyes and calmed his breathing to bring his mind and body as close as possible to becoming one. A few minutes passed, and he stood almost completely motionless. Finally, he stopped any movement in his body and felt at one with himself. In that instance, he sent his left fist flying toward the gate. On contact, a loud sound was heard like a bomb had gone off. The gate caved in, came off the wall, flew several meters away, and crashed to the ground.

The Immortal Slave walked through the entrance he had created and looked around.

Close by, there were almost a hundred guards and a few influential people seated at tables and chairs. Many were standing up and visibly startled by what had transpired. The Immortal Slave looked around and was happy to see that Min's intel had been correct. He had destroyed the gate right next to where the overseer's son's birthday was being held.

Making sure to sell his role as a Deep Snow clan warrior, he screamed in their language, "Death to the City of Noel!"

While many people were stunned by this sudden appearance, a voice called out to the people, "Everyone, don't back down no matter who we are facing. We are the City of Noel and have been butchering Deep Snow filth for over two hundred years."

Who was brave enough to draw attention to themself in this situation? It was the overseer's son, Robert Ruffin Barrow. He was a lean teenager with dark brown hair. He wore a 19th-century style Edwardian suit that seemed to be made of tier-two source thread, one of the best materials for strengthening the body and increasing power for someone in the second tier. With green eyes the color of money, he saw everything in front of him as his property. The arrogance in his eyes was the same as the first time the Immortal Slave saw him all those years ago.

After Robert spoke up, the guards in the area improved their attitudes. Almost all of them stood up and began surrounding the enemy as he started making his way toward them. The Immortal Slave didn't even look at the guards. As soon as he saw Robert, his eyes never left the young man, as if looking away would make him disappear.

The Immortal Slave remembered his first and only meeting with Robert. He became filled with fury that all he had done back then was break one of Robert's teeth with a punch after the pompous asshole whipped an older woman named Akira half to death. As far as the Immortal Slave knew, Akira died a few days later due to complications from her injuries. That was one of the most vivid memories the Immortal Slave held in his mind. At first, he wanted nothing more than to rip off Robert's arms and limbs. *Piece of shit,* he thought to himself. Still, he knew that if he lost control, the plan wouldn't go the way they wanted. So, he reined in his emotions and focused on the task.

Being inside the second layer of the city's defenses, the Immortal Slave was surrounded by nothing but tier-two source users. Almost all of them had already materialized their weapons and were waiting for the order to move. Next to Robert were some hooded people who weren't releasing any form of energy out of their bodies. Due to the Immortal Slave's sharp senses, not knowing who the mystery people were was the most disturbing part of the situation.

Once Robert gave the order to kill the enemy, the guards took their positions and used their training tactics to fight. The first guard to reach the Immortal Slave was a second-level mid-tier peak source user. His weapon was a bastard sword, and his element was earth. He jumped high in the air and added the earth to his weapon to make it heavier. Coming down with incredible speed, he aimed for the head of the Immortal Slave, but in the blink of an eye, the guard couldn't find him. When the guard looked to his left, he wasn't prepared for what came next. From his right, a fist flew in the direction of his head, sending him flying toward one of the walls by the broken gate. Since the gate and walls were connected through a source formation, the walls were greatly weakened once the gate had been broken. So, the guard had become the first hole in the wall, but he certainly wasn't going to be the last.

Quickly, the guards remembered how this lone enemy had broken the gate. From that alone, the guards thought the Immortal Slave had enough power to be compared to a peak tier-two source user. They underestimated their opponent the first time because they hadn't seen him holding a weapon. It was the first time most of them ever saw someone fight without a weapon. Scared, the guards didn't know what to do.

The most powerful people the guards knew were the overseers, and their powers were at least second-tier upper-primary level. Even Rod, Robert's father, didn't move forward, seeming as if he didn't know what to do. Seeing that he had frightened everyone present in the room, the Immortal Slave then called out in the Deep Snow clan's language, "Look at all of you! Too scared to face an enemy that has broken into your home. You better stop me from leaving, or I swear, I will come back in three months and bring a group as strong as myself and tear this city to the ground."

He turned around and started to move back the way he came but not too fast so that the fear of an even more powerful assault would shortly draw the guards to attempt to stop him.

Then, when they couldn't stop him, they would spend the next three months wasting time getting ready for his return. Once they realized he would never come back, the guards would go to the Deep Snow clan and begin a war that would hopefully destroy all of them. The city that lives off the lives of slaves and a clan that makes their living off stealing said slaves and selling them to other clans for profit would both cease to exist.

The Immortal Slave thought his plan was perfect, but in the next moment, everything he had carefully crafted came crashing down.

"Where the hell do you think you are going, Daisuke?"

Startled beyond measure, the Immortal Slave, whose real name is Daisuke, stopped immediately and looked toward the main stage. Standing there with an evil grin on his face was Robert. He had called the Immortal Slave by his given name—a name he hadn't heard since his family lost everything. The Immortal Slave stood in place, running scenarios through his head to figure out what went wrong. Giving their opponent no time to think, one of the hooded figures next to Robert took a low stance and drew back a longbow that was hidden under their hood.

When the figure released the arrow, it moved at an unbelievably fast speed. Without warning, the arrow pierced the mask the Immortal Slave used to hide his face. In the next moment, the arrow was stuck in the ground with the mask. If not for the Immortal Slave's fast reflexes, his right cheek would have had a hole through it.

The surrounding guards were shocked that a slave was the one who had caused so much damage to the city. They began to wonder how he could have gotten so powerful under their noses. No longer able to maintain his façade, the Immortal Slave began answering by his given name, Daisuke.

While the guards were experiencing a rollercoaster of emotions, Daisuke wasn't faring any better. After dodging the longbow's arrow, Daisuke was still in a panic. Two thoughts occupied his mind: how Robert knew he was causing all the destruction before he lost his mask and how the hooded figure generated so much power without concentrating their source energy first. Typically, people who followed the way of the spirit harnessed their energy by first gathering it before releasing it all at once, but the way the hooded figure did it was too similar to something Daisuke felt he recognized but couldn't put his finger on.

Meanwhile, Robert didn't give his opponent any time to think or plan. His next words caused Daisuke's brain to shut off its logical side and act on pure instinct. "Think you can just walk in here, destroy the place, and leave to go hopping around in the wasteland with the rest of your trash?" Robert taunted.

Once Daisuke heard that, his mind was full of terror. He realized his enemy knew his plans. Feeling naked and trapped with no way out, Daisuke asked, "How did you know about all of this?"

Robert walked to the center of the stage, and with an evil grin, he snapped his fingers. At that signal, the hooded figures spread out slowly across the room. Daisuke saw something horrifying once they were out of the way. Chained to several posts, Min and Weakness had been cruelly beaten and heavily injured. Min's arms were chained above her head and Weakness's arm and legs were chained down. They were both barely conscious.

At that moment, Daisuke lost all sense of himself and let out the loudest yell he could. "NOOOOO!"

Forsaking his original plan, Daisuke headed straight to where the two most important people in his life were. Any guard that was in his path was instantly destroyed with a punch, breaking both of their arms in an attempt to block his attack or being smashed into the ground and enduring a severe blow to the head. The guards who jumped at Daisuke to try and sneak attack him were grabbed and sent flying through a nearby wall, creating dozens of holes in the structure.

Daisuke moved like a bat out of hell. Nothing could get in his way. Once he reached the stage, the hooded figures aimed their attacks toward him. Four dashed directly at him and swung their fists in his direction. Without thinking, Daisuke's body instinctively knew something was wrong. He hadn't seen anyone else in the entire region, other than himself, use their bare hands in a fight before. Once the four figures struck Daisuke's cross-arm block, he was forced to back up several feet. Suddenly, another terrifying realization came over Daisuke: the hooded figures were using their bodies' physical strength to attack him, which was not the way of spirit source-based attacks to be used.

Because they were using the same body fighting method as him, Daisuke was filled with more unanswered questions. He thought, *How had they learned this method*? As far as he knew, there was no method in the city to cultivate this kind of strength, and the only way he had learned it was from hearing the special mantra from Weakness's mouth all those years ago.

Daisuke knew that being unfocused was causing his re-action time to slow down, so he decided to stop thinking about those things so that he could get to where he had to be. Even though the hooded figures had comparable physical strength to his, it was clear that they weren't on his level yet. He increased his speed and attacked the hooded figures one by one. Before the rest were able to bring out their hidden weapons, he focused as much strength as he could muster into one fist and punched some of them so hard that they were smashed into the ground and sank in the ground like it was mud.

The first hooded figure to attack him was specially targeted because Daisuke feared long-range attacks more than any. So, with an uppercut blocked by their sturdy bow, the hooded figure was sent soaring into the distance. After taking care of a few of them, the rest seemed less confident that they could take Daisuke on.

He made his way toward the center of the stage to attack Robert with a quick jab to the chest. At that moment, all he wanted to do was rip out Robert's heart. However, when Daisuke sent out his attack, Robert surprisingly also sent out a powerful kick aimed at Daisuke's groin. Both blocked each other's attack, and from that exchange, Daisuke made a horrifying realization that both had around the same level of physical power.

Robert kept smiling and looked down at Daisuke. "Is this all the power you can bring out? I was expecting something I couldn't handle on my own. To think, what took you six years of training and hiding to do, I completed within two years."

Daisuke finally lost all hope of winning to fight someone else of the same caliber as him.

While surrounded by tough opponents left and right, he didn't see any hope of getting out of there without sacrificing his girlfriend and best friend. However, he shook his head to clear his thoughts. Daisuke didn't see a life without Min or Weakness as worth living, so he focused on what he could do at that moment: reach them and keep making steps as he went along.

Daisuke made a mad dash toward Min and Weakness, but as if expecting his movements, Robert intercepted his enemy. Daisuke knew he had to take risks, so he aimed a full powerful-powered punch at Robert's side. Instead of attacking,

Robert tried to block as much of the attack's power as possible to neutralize it from damaging the area around him. While Robert was momentarily in one place, Daisuke reached Min and Weakness. He easily crushed the chains that held his unconscious girlfriend bound, then quickly laid her down. Daisuke tried to break the chains that held Weakness, but they were harder to crush than the gate he had just destroyed.

He thought, *Why were Min's chains so easy to break but Weakness's chains seemingly made of the toughest materials I have ever touched or seen in my twelve years as a slave?*

With no time to seriously contemplate his question, Daisuke heard a sharp whistling sound. He looked away from Weakness's chains and saw the hooded figure with the longbow had made its way back toward him and shot an arrow directly at Min, who was still unconscious. Without even thinking, Daisuke moved to block the arrow from hitting Min. While moving with moderate effort, Daisuke caught the arrow in mid-air and saved Min . . . or so he thought.

Suddenly, Daisuke felt a dull pain in his left side. He was beyond shocked. His senses were so heightened that he could react to almost any stimuli in his area of perception, but there was an exception.

Whenever Daisuke believed there could be no danger coming from a place he had deemed safe, his senses ignored the usual warnings of the unknown coming at him. Because of this, he looked down and saw a beautifully designed serpent-shaped dagger coming out of both sides of his abdomen. Unsure of how he was stabbed, Daisuke's mind quickly tried to discover the culprits using the process of elimination. He arrived at only one conclusion.

Daisuke turned his neck to see Min with a sinister smile that didn't even look human. She removed her hands from the dagger and quickly jumped away from Daisuke. Daisuke's mind raced as he tried to make sense of what had happened. Attempting to move toward Min, he took a step forward. But when his foot hit the ground, his vision became blurry, and he felt all his strength leave him.

"WHAT THE HELL IS GOING ON?" Daisuke uttered with what little energy he had left.

Chapter Four
The Ugly Truth

D aisuke was intelligent and strong, so no matter how strong his body became, he made sure to never neglect his mind's growth. While he hadn't had a formal education since he was five years old, he traded hard labor with other slaves in exchange for them teaching him. From knowledge about plants to combat and strategy, he learned from anyone willing to teach him.

When that was no longer enough, he allowed himself to be used as target practice for the guards so that he could watch them during their classes and absorb as much information as he could. After twelve years of this, he was able to use his knowledge to formulate a plan of escape for not only himself but also as many people as he could take with him. However, throughout all those years, he was never able to learn one of the most brutal truths to swallow: don't trust anyone. When you do, you will be left caught in a trap of your own making.

After being stabbed by the person he trusted the most in this world, Daisuke found it hard to even move. His mind was in complete chaos, and his usual quick-witted-and-always-advancing mentality was stuck in the mud. Nothing made sense to him anymore. He only kept wondering why. *Why was this happening? Why did Min stab him? Why wasn't he able to move?* All these questions kept bouncing around his mind. But no matter how many times he asked, his mind couldn't give him any answers.

After being stabbed, all his strength left him. It was as if he had never been strong in the first place. Even holding his body up was too difficult, and after a few moments, he dropped to his knees until he completely collapsed to the ground face first. Once that happened, a maniacal laugh began reverberating throughout the area.

"I can't believe it was this easy to destroy you. I spent so much time and effort preparing for this day, but once it came, I wasn't even needed to bring you down," said Robert.

Walking over to Daisuke's best friend, Weakness, Robert smiled from ear to ear, enjoying the sense of superiority he felt. With another snap of his fingers, the hooded figures moved over to pick Daisuke up. Once in their hands, they took him to the post Min had been tied to and removed the chains that were around Weakness's arm and legs. Then, they bound Daisuke's legs and arms with those same chains to the vacant post and forcibly put him in a kneeling position.

Once finished, Robert sat down in front of Daisuke in the golden chair he had made for this occasion. It was as if he was an emperor addressing his subjects. The whole time, Daisuke had a frantic look in his eyes, but his gaze wasn't directed at anything. He looked like he was searching for an answer to all the questions in his head.

Once Robert had had enough of Daisuke's pain, he threw out a question to him so they could continue with the show. "Do you regret it now, filth? Putting your hands on your better all those years ago?"

Although weak and unable to move, Daisuke remained defiant and didn't answer Robert's question. Instead, he asked, "What did you do to my Min?"

Surprised that, even after being stabbed in the back, Daisuke's first concern was for Min, Robert momentarily felt bad for the slave. He began laughing even harder. "Wow, she had you wrapped around her finger more than I thought. Truly magnificent work, baby."

At first, Daisuke couldn't figure out who Robert was calling "baby," but the next words he heard shattered his heart.

"Why, of course, these slaves are so slow-witted and foolish that pulling the wool over their eyes is child's play."

Startled by what he'd heard, Daisuke recognized the voice. He struggled to turn his head, but after much exhausting effort, he saw Min coming from a changing area. No longer in rags and looking beaten, he saw her flawless skin with no bruises or blemishes. She was wearing a beautiful Qing dynasty Hanfu made from the same quality source thread as Robert's clothes. On her outfit was a design pattern of a great and evil serpent with green and gold skin.

Gracefully walking over to them, Min smiled brightly. It was the same smile she had shown Daisuke earlier that day. Once she reached them, she sat down in Robert's lap and deeply kissed him in front of Daisuke. With a pained look that couldn't make sense of anything, Daisuke's mind tried to rationalize what was going on. But he couldn't.

With nothing else to do but break down on the inside, Daisuke asked, "Why? Why would you, of all people, betray me?"

"Haha, silly slave. I never betrayed you. To betray someone, you would have to actually be on their side," said Min with a new cruel look. The kind, gentle girl Daisuke knew before was replaced with an arrogant, evil monster of a woman who seemed to take pleasure in Daisuke's pain.

Even while crushed on the inside and feeling a sense of pain he had never felt before, Daisuke managed to push those feelings down slightly and ask, "What do you mean?"

Robert, reveling in Daisuke's anguish, looked him dead in the eyes and dropped a truth bomb on him. "The person you call Min has never existed. Her real name is Lü Zhi. She was being honest when she told you that she became a slave after her family's kingdom was overthrown, but that's it. I met her three years ago when I was on a trip to gather slaves with my father, and when our eyes met, I could see the same look in her eyes that I had. Even when in bondage, she knew that almost everyone else was beneath her, and just being called a slave, she almost killed me. But that fire inside her led to us falling in love. So, while on our way back, we came up with this amazing plan together. At first, I just wanted to mess with your emotions and head to get back at you. But who knew that you had this amazing technique for strengthening your body? Did you think we kept you alive because you were strong? The only reason you are alive is that we were waiting for you to give her the rest of the technique so we could make our bodies as strong as level three. But after so much time, we realized that you didn't have it."

Daisuke reeled after hearing Robert's words. Once the truth came out, his mind was finally not as messy as it had been moments ago, but it only worsened the pain in his chest. Seeing Daisuke in shock, Robert was filled with euphoria. For so many years, he had felt so inferior compared to Daisuke that the feelings haunted him. But after taking down his greatest foe, Robert was on top of the world.

To drive the knife deeper into Daisuke, Robert revealed his plans. "Just so you know, our master, The Merchant, has known about you for years. He told me that being at level three as a way of the spirit user. He was able to sense how source energy moved in the area, and with your body absorbing it over all these years, he would have had to be blind and dumb not to notice that you became a peak tier-two source user."

Daisuke trembled after hearing this. For many years, he thought he had kept his real strength hidden, but to his surprise, he was dancing in the palm of The Merchant's hand the whole time.

Robert continued to pile more horrible information on top of Daisuke's head. "The reason you can't move is because we used Lü Zhi's way of the spirit ability to poison you. You see, her ability to generate poison is dangerous to anyone who uses source energy. It prevents them from circulating source energy through their body or spirit, so all of your strength is now gone forever."

Daisuke didn't say anything, which truly made Robert angry. Lü Zhi's poison was more powerful when used by a stronger person. It should have only worked for the next half hour based on when Robert tested it on himself. Robert lay in hopes of crushing Daisuke's will and turning him into a puppet that couldn't defy his orders, just like the hooded figures Robert kept at his side. But Daisuke had a stronger will than Robert expected, so he had one last plan left.

"I heard that you have been in constant pain over not being able to protect your best friend from being neutered all those years ago and that you were looking for the person who did that," said Robert.

As if a fire had been lit inside Daisuke, a light burned in his eyes as his look of sorrow was replaced with fury. "It was you, you son of a bitch, wasn't it?" Daisuke fumed with rage.

Happy that he got a reaction out of his opponent, Robert continued speaking. "No, not me. You see, I just wanted to kill your friend and leave you to only depend on Lü Zhi, but someone else had an even better idea. What would be crueler? To leave you all alone except for one person or to mutilate one of the only people you care about and have that guilt of not protecting them eat at you daily?"

Daisuke went from rage to despair within moments, and he finally lost all composure. "It can't be." Daisuke turned his gaze from Robert to Lü Zhi, the woman he used to call "Min."

After being betrayed by her, in the back of Daisuke's mind, he held hope that Robert had just manipulated her and that she was the girl that he'd fallen in love with. Upon hearing the truth that she was behind the monstrous act that befell Weakness, all feelings of love were replaced with many conflicting emotions of sadness, anger, self-hatred, and despair.

Seeing that Daisuke didn't want to admit to himself that it was true, Lü Zhi began to speak. "Do you remember the day you had asked me to look over him while you were away for a task? When you came back, I was bawling my eyes out. I told you a story about how two masked men came in and cut him in front of me, but the amazing truth was that it was me. I laughed the whole time I was cutting him. I wanted to see a reaction out of that emotionless slave, but I didn't get anything from him. It made me so mad that I changed my plan of just removing the balls and taking the trunk with it. To prove it, I got Robert to get me a special storage device so I could preserve my work."

Pulling out a special pouch, Lü Zhi sent source energy into it, creating a hole in the air the size of a bookshelf that sent something out of it. Out on the floor lay Daisuke's best friend's genitals encased in a protective hunting case. Having grown up with Weakness most of his life, Daisuke recognized his best friend's genitalia. He had no more doubt that the monster in front of him had done the unspeakable to someone he considered family.

Chapter Five

No Hope Left

D aisuke lost it. He started to utter a sound so terrifying that it created fear within anyone nearby who was below his level of power. Robert and Lü Zhi were startled by the abrupt burst of power. They were expecting to crush Daisuke's spirit, allowing them to use The Merchant's formation technique to put him under a seal that would force him to follow all their commands. Instead, Daisuke was able to overcome the poison by forcing his body's source energy to flow faster and at a greater volume than ever before.

Having been near the peak of level two for five months, possessing only the mantra for power up to the peak of level two and only being self-taught with no special supplies to help his power grow fast, Daisuke shouldn't have been able to make a breakthrough to a level of power he didn't have the method to reach. Still, the intense emotions raging inside him to get out created a path for his body to do the impossible and begin to reach level three.

With no time to waste, Daisuke stood up and pulled against his chains. He saw Robert and Lü Zhi grow pale, not expecting this turn of events. The only time the two had ever felt this level of power in the city was with only a few other people, but they were scared to compare Daisuke to those people.

Sounds of grinding metal began to echo as Daisuke put all his energy into getting his hands on the two people in front of him. Robert and Lü Zhi quickly backed away from Daisuke and cried out for the guards and the hooded figures to return to subdue Daisuke before he could break free.

The crowd, which had been silent until this moment, was scared of the unexpected change in plans. Robert had a group of people there to witness his demonstration of subjugating the strongest slave in the city, finally proving that he was worthy of being an overseer like his father. To their surprise, it was clear that Robert no longer had a grasp on the situation. People began to run for the exits, and chaos ensued as Daisuke grew closer to a new height of power.

While the guards and hooded figures tried to stop Daisuke, it was like trying to put out a burning house with a cup of water. All of their blows didn't make him flinch when they landed on him, and even the arrows that were previously a danger to him a few minutes prior were barely able to pierce his skin. As the seconds counted down, Daisuke got closer and closer to breaking free. At that moment, Daisuke was drunk on his power, thinking he could crush his enemies with a wave of his hand.

Finally, the moment came for him to break his chains. But suddenly, in the sky right above the city, the word βάρος appeared in massive letters the size of a building and fell on Daisuke. Crushed by the surprised attack, Daisuke found himself slightly buried in the ground with blood flowing from his new wounds and several of his bones shattered. No longer having the power to resist due to all his source energy being knocked out of him, Daisuke was without any other means to turn the situation around.

After a few seconds, the massive word disappeared, and out from the crowd, a plum middle-aged man dressed in extravagantly fine clothing began to slowly walk toward Robert, Lü Zhi, and Daisuke.

Upon recognizing the man, Robert and Lü Zhi got down on one knee and bowed. "We pay respect to the master," they said in unison.

Upon reaching them, the man, Edward Colston, also known as "The Merchant," looked down at Robert and said, "I can't believe that I had to intervene to stop this slave from causing a mess." The Merchant continued, "I have high hopes for you, my boy. If I didn't have to intervene and you had put this slave under control, you could have been one of my most esteemed overseers by passing this test. But seeing how you weren't able to prepare enough so that any surprise wouldn't have thrown your plan into disorder, you aren't ready enough."

Seeing the disappointment in The Merchant's eyes, Robert touched his forehead to the ground and said, "I am deeply ashamed of myself, sir. No excuse can pardon me for my grave mistake. I will accept any punishment that you see fit."

From disappointment to joy, The Merchant's facial expression changed as he reveled in the personal growth he felt Robert had just gone through. "Enough. The fact that you have accepted your mistake is enough for me. This mere slave isn't worthy of you receiving a punishment," said The Merchant.

Robert was delighted. Ever since he was a child, The Merchant had always been nice to him. He had learned the joys of dominating others by watching them grovel at The Merchant's feet.

Robert never understood why The Merchant was so good to him. He always assumed it was because they had the same source weapon and element ability. While it wasn't uncommon for people to share one of those abilities, it was scarce for people to share both simultaneously.

While those thoughts went through Robert's mind, The Merchant looked at Lü Zhi and said, "Even though the plan didn't completely work, we still were able to turn this problem into a gain. Seeing how this slave was able to almost reach level three with just his emotions running wild, we now have a solution to reaching even greater power. With you by Robert's side, I have full confidence that you will go far. But take this as a lesson to never relax until the job is fully done."

"Understood, Master," said Lü Zhi with her eyes still aimed at the ground. Unlike Robert,

she had no relationship with The Merchant. This was the first time he had ever been this close to her, so she knew not to make any mistakes in front of him because they wouldn't be tolerated.

Seeing how smart Lü Zhi was and knowing that she knew the best way to interact with people above her, The Merchant was satisfied that she would make a good wife for Robert.

"Since you have completed your task, I can now tell you that I have found the remnants of your family hiding and plotting to take back their kingdom because I knew neither of you would fail me. I have already contacted them, and we will be able to ally with them once they arrive to come to see you."

Lü Zhi was visibly startled by this news. For so long, she had only been able to act like she was a noble ever since the revolt happened, but now that everything she was supposed to have was finally within reach, she couldn't do anything but smile. She smiled the same smile she had shown Daisuke earlier in the morning.

After The Merchant finished speaking to Robert and Lü Zhi, he turned his gaze to Daisuke, who was still slightly buried in the ground. With a flick of The Merchant's wrist, the wind dug Daisuke out of the ground and brought his head up, forcing him to look The Merchant directly in his eyes.

"Wow. I'll admit, out of all the slaves I have sold, killed, raped, or tortured, you are the most impressive one I have ever seen," said The Merchant. "When I first found out about you and your special mantra, I was just going to torture you till you told me where you were able to acquire it. Then, I was going to throw you away or turn you into a mindless puppet. But honestly, I wasn't in a rush to get the truth, so I thought this would be a great trial for Robert. I have wanted to kill you in the cruelest way possible since you put your dirty hands on Robert all those years ago, but my father always taught me that a man has to handle his problems if he wants to go far in this world. So, I allowed you to be. Even I was surprised when you were on the verge of reaching such a high level of power, so I had to step in before things got too difficult for Robert. Now I will do this my way. Robert only has the seal that will make you spill all your secrets if you lose all will to fight, but I am a powerful formation user. My ability is strong enough to get all I need out of you without any restrictions. I'll tell you what, if you tell me where you got the mantra, I'll allow you to keep your mind and make you a puppet with some level of free will to think. What you say, boy?"

With blood trickling down Daisuke's head and covering his left eye, he struggled to stay conscious and muster one of the last ounces of strength he had left. Tilting his head toward The Merchant, he said, "Go fuck yourself! Your whole family can burn in hell!"

The Merchant chuckled out loud and replied, "You have spirit. I'll give you that. But honestly, even if you had agreed, I would have still killed you as soon as I had what I wanted because I won't let an enemy survive for too long under my control."

Reaching out his hand toward Daisuke, The Merchant used his source energy to form the word δοῦλος on his palm. "Say goodbye to your last moments of consciousness, you piece of filth," said The Merchant.

Thinking back on his whole life, Daisuke was filled with regret—losing his family and kingdom due to being a power-less child, all those years of enslavement, falling for a spy and then being betrayed by her. Each memory stung, but in what he thought were his last moments, his biggest regret was not being able to repay the favor Weakness had done for him all those years ago.

Despite the exhaustion weighing heavily upon him, Daisuke managed to muster the strength to turn his head and direct his gaze towards his best friend, now free from the chains that had been removed and transferred onto Daisuke himself. He stood unencumbered, liberated from the burdens that once bound him. He wanted the last image in his head to be the sight of his best friend.

Startled, he saw no one. There was no sign that Weakness had ever been in that area in the first place.

While Daisuke was deeply confused and racking his brain, The Merchant finished creating his enslavement formation on his hand and started moving his hand to place the symbol on Daisuke's forehead. As he was about to touch Daisuke, The Merchant felt a change in the environment. It was as if space itself had suddenly vanished. Startled, he stopped and looked around to figure out what was happening.

Out of thin air, a young man appeared behind The Merchant. With only one arm, this man created a violet-black sword and yelled to the sky as if people could see him. "TRY AND KILL ME NOW, YOU BASTARDS!"

Once the sword appeared, the sky went dark as it became filled with clouds. From the biggest cloud descended a lightning bolt aimed at the young man who had been yelling. At the same moment the lightning bolt reached him, he ran his sword through The Merchant's back.

Chapter Six

Our Protagonist Appears

The Merchant was a cruel man whose family has a deep history of selling people into slavery. Although he wasn't the most powerful family member, he was still formidable due to his ability to generate revenue and create lower-tier formations. Unlike his older brother, he wasn't a highly skilled fighter. Still, due to his brother's reputation, protection, and connections, The Merchant was able to take over the city and become the biggest frog in a small pond with no one within a close distance being able to match his level of power.

With no one to challenge his dominance, he had no need to anticipate surprise attacks. Due to that, he was completely unprepared for the attack coming out of nowhere from the one-armed enemy.

As the sword ran through him, The Merchant felt an intense jolt of pain. Without warning, he felt his core source energy being drawn out of him. Though injured, he was surprisingly lucky that the sword only nicked a part of his source core, or the place in all things that utilized source energy and held the user's power to absorb source energy. With his source core being damaged, The Merchant found his power instantly drop from tier-three mid-level to tier three primary.

Feeling his core almost destroyed, The Merchant immediately created a wind blast that separated him from his attacker. With the force from that blast moving him away from his attacker, The Merchant felt safer and started to assess the situation while a small amount of blood started to pool underneath him. He looked at the person who attacked him and was truly startled. In front of him was one of the slaves he had owned for years. With only one eye, one arm, countless scars, and a skinny frame, the slave looked like he wouldn't have the strength to even pick up the black sword he was holding. But when The Merchant saw the gaze the slave gave off and the presence he held, he couldn't help but shudder at the intensity of it all.

The Merchant couldn't process what was happening. After all his talk to Robert about not letting his guard down until he had completed the task, The Merchant found himself having fallen short. Trying to make sense of what was going on, The Merchant, Robert, Lü Zhi, Robert's father Rod, and all the guards in the area found themselves confused and unable to handle the new development. The slave known as Weakness had always been an absent-minded good-for-nothing since he was brought to the city twelve years earlier, yet he stood right in front of them with his back and head held high as if to not let anyone look down on him.

While the crowd was trying to figure out what was going on, with anger, Weakness thought, *So many years of pain, humiliation, torture, and planning down the drain. I wasn't even able to destroy that piece of shit's source core. FUCK! I truly thought with his mind on trying to enslave Daisuke, I would have been able to get that fucker by channeling the lightning tribulation through my body and sword and bring an end to this nightmare. But when I moved through the void and momentarily opened it up briefly to surprise attack him, I wasn't able to hide the absence of space, which alerted him and led me to miss my mark.*

After figuring out his mistake, Weakness changed gears and focused on plan B. He started running toward The Merchant and drawing in massive amounts of source energy from his surroundings to strengthen his black sword. While it was unnatural for a regular human to bring down a lightning tribulation before they break through to tier-six, he could still store that energy and use it to help his cultivation.

With typical beginner tier-one spirit source users, the only thing they can do is create their source item. In the beginning, they are only able to hold its form for a few seconds at best. As they get better and can hold it longer, the more real it becomes and the higher the realm they can reach in tier-one. Once they reach a minute or can faintly see the item, they have broken through the primary realm. As soon as the item looks translucent, usually within an hour, they know they have broken through the mid-tier realm. After a day, or once the item looks close to being real, they will reach the upper tier realm. Finally, when they can hold its form indefinitely, or it is no different than a tangible item, they have reached the pinnacle level of tier-one realm and are ready to challenge tier-two. However, Weakness's sword and his cultivation method threw that notion out the window and was unlike anything anyone had ever seen.

As soon as Weakness started making his way toward The Merchant, everyone in the area was jolted from their confusion. The only thought on most of their minds was to protect their master. The first one to move was The Merchant. While he was still scared of Weakness's unknown ability, he swiftly started gathering his source energy and changed it so he could create wind blades with peak tier-two amounts of power in each one using twenty-five percent of the energy in his body. Almost simultaneously, Robert generated his spirit halberd and wrapped it in wind. With his way of the body source energy being at peak level two with one step, he rushed forward and appeared behind Weakness to cut him in half.

With both attacks bearing down on him, Weakness didn't spare a glance. He disappeared, which caused Robert to find himself in the path of multiple peak tier-two wind blades quickly descending upon him. While Robert had the body of peak level two, he didn't train himself as well as Daisuke, so he couldn't react fast enough to dodge the attacks. The Merchant was surprised, so he didn't have enough time to control his fastest attack, leading to him helplessly watching as Robert became deeply wounded. The Merchant felt his heart rip out of his body as he saw Robert's blood spill out.

The Merchant and Robert's father, Rod, were both unsettled by what had just happened.

They rushed to Robert's side and started calling out as he fell unconscious from the heavy wounds. With their attention fully focused on Robert, they didn't see Weakness reappear behind one of the guards. The moment he reappeared, Weakness's sword went flying toward the guard's vitals.

Weakness quietly said to himself, "More."

With a quick stab, the guard found his heart skewered by Weakness's black-bladed shirasaya katana with a silver handle and sheath tied to his side. Coughing up blood, a look of surprise was plastered on the guard's face.

Behind him, Weakness said in a low voice, "All these years, I've watched as you pieces of shit committed all sorts of unforgivable sins with no idea that one day I would pass judgment on you. Well, the day has come. Because your crimes were on the low side, I grant you mercy by killing you quickly. But know that the worst of your kind won't have an easy death. I can promise you that."

With a quick pull, he retracted his blade from the guard's back, and as his body dropped to the floor, Weakness disappeared once again. The Merchant shot more wind blades toward Weakness's direction but was unable to put a scratch on his enemy.

The Merchant ordered his guards to group up and watch each other's backs. The Merchant slowly started to panic. When he first found out about Daisuke's power, he was startled because he had never used his source sense technique to check out the slaves. To save face, he acted as if he knew the whole time so as not to embarrass himself in front of Robert and Lü Zhi. After that, he made sure to have a full grasp on what was going on in his city so that he would not be caught off guard again. But all his planning fell short when Weakness literally stabbed him in the back, almost destroying his cultivation in one go.

Seeing himself and his men helpless in the face of this attack, The Merchant tried to find a way to end things quickly. But he knew nothing about Weakness, so he couldn't formulate a plan to deal with his opponent's disappearing act.

Suddenly, The Merchant heard Lü Zhi yell, "Stop, you filth! Or I'll cut this worthless slave's throat right now."

The Merchant turned toward Lü Zhi and saw her holding an unconscious Daisuke by the hair—the dagger she had used to stab him held against his throat. Weakness stopped moving for a moment with his back to Lü Zhi. His sword was touching the back of another guard.

Lü Zhi was happy to see her scheme had paid off, even though she feared how well Weakness had hidden his true self. She knew most people wouldn't be able to throw away the person who cared for them for so many years. The Merchant, seeing that Weakness was finally staying in one place, sent casual wind blades his way while the guard moved away as fast as he could, expecting Weakness to vanish as he had done before.

The Merchant started looking around to see where Weakness could appear. Instead, the wind blades left deep cuts on Weakness's body. Rather than screaming or even making any noise, Weakness closed his eyes and stayed motionless.

Believing that she had won, Lü Zhi started laughing at both Daisuke and Weakness. "Even though you were able to trick us with your actions, you were still caught because of your inferior mind and inability to throw away those who can bring you down. I promise you that The Merchant and I will kill you miserably."

While being hit constantly by wind blades, Weakness didn't do anything besides protect his vitals with his special ability and let his sword absorb all the source energy he had stolen from the people he'd killed. Seeing that his attacks were hitting Weakness, The Merchant decided to go all out and use the strongest attack he could pull off with his source core being temporarily damaged. He created a formation seal in his hand with "κόβω," the ancient Greek symbol for cut, to increase the cutting power in his seal. Then, he gathered as much source energy as he could handle and transformed it into the wind. By fusing them together, he took his power up to another level to finish Weakness off once and for all.

Silently standing in front of his opponent, Weakness showed no signs of concern for what was happening around him. His mind was moving as quickly as possible to reach his goal. At level one, a person is trained to feel the source energy inside of them and materialize it into an item, the duration of its lasting is the usual indicator to show what realm they have reached, so when there is no energy loss in using it, that is when they have reached the pinnacle of level one and are ready to start approaching level two.

At that moment, Weakness had accumulated enough of the stolen energy to properly imitate tier-one spirit source energy to reach level one pinnacle within those few minutes of fighting. He was anything but done. He pressured his muscles with source energy to strengthen his body as quickly as possible, then he caused all the muscles in his body to rip apart and heal over and over again.

Usually, it would be impossible for someone to use two different cultivation techniques simultaneously, especially from two different paths. Still, Weakness's special ability helped him do the impossible. No one else wanted to be anywhere near Weakness or The Merchant, so people started running away, once again, from the area. The Merchant opened his hands outward to reveal a thin line of space cutting everything in its path. This was his tier-three primary wind formation technique, Space Cutter, with the power to cut a building in half.

With the cutter inching toward his face, Weakness showed no signs of moving. He opened his eye to see a bolt of lightning from the sky had struck him once again. Even bigger and darker clouds gathered overhead.

Noticing the scene's similarity to Weakness's ambush earlier, Lü Zhi realized that Weakness was in the exact spot and position he was in when he stabbed The Merchant in the back and had called lightning down the first time. She didn't know why this was important, but she felt it was critical.

With the lightning being faster than the wind, Weakness's body was energized by the familiar feeling of his whole existence being supercharged with a battery of infinite power.

Weakness didn't move from his spot because he knew his opponents would use Daisuke

against him at some point, so he kept his eye on Daisuke the whole time when Lü Zhi was reaching for Daisuke's head. Weakness targeted the guard that was at that exact spot at the time.

Since his first plan to kill The Merchant with a surprise attack failed, Weakness proceeded to plan B, which was to steal enough power from the guards' cores to break through the same spot he had the first time. Doing it in the same spot made that place the cultivator's holy land, greatly benefiting their abilities. With the power from his new holy land, Weakness's tier-two power and absorbed energy from the lightning tribulation gave him enough energy to reach tier-two upper pinnacle. Still, his whole being was already drained and worn out from the quick, continuous fashion breakthroughs, so he knew he couldn't take The Merchant's attack head-on.

The wind blade line split Weakness in half, and his body fell apart. When Lü Zhi started to giggle to herself about Weakness being dead, she realized that a shadowy figure had been split. The Merchant was furious that he couldn't kill a tiny slave like Weakness, so he quickly ordered Lü

Zhi to kill Daisuke. Lü Zhi was momentarily startled that her plan fell through, but she quickly lunged her dagger at Daisuke's throat. However, before her dagger could penetrate his throat, Daisuke disappeared.

Surprised that both Weakness and Daisuke were gone, everyone began searching for their bodies. They were scared that they were next. After a few seconds, Weakness reappeared near Lü Zhi and tried to stab her in the stomach. Since Lü Zhi wasn't as powerful as Daisuke, she didn't have the endurance to keep her way of the body always up or drive her way of the spirit power to keep her source clothes on defense mode all the time. So, Weakness finally had the chance to harm the woman he hated most in the world. However, since she was still more powerful than him in both body and spirit, he couldn't appear right next to her.

After reappearing, Weakness moved at almost the same speed as before, with his sword aiming to cause major damage. Unlike the people who Weakness had killed before, Lü Zhi had enough time to avoid Weakness's weapon. With her spirit dagger materializing in her open hand, Lü Zhi was able to make sure the blade never touched her. However, while her attention was on the sword, Lü Zhi didn't notice Weakness's flying kick aiming straight for her stomach.

With Weakness's kick bouncing off Lü Zhi's flesh, everyone in the area thought Weakness wasn't strong enough without the sword to do any damage. But only he knew how vicious and cruel his attack was.

After disappearing again to avoid Lü Zhi's counterattack, Weakness appeared next to the protective hunting case that contained his genitals. Once he placed his hand on the case, the whole thing disappeared. By gaining the case, Weakness was finally able to release the tension from his body, and in that moment of relaxation, he almost lost consciousness. But he held on through sheer willpower while almost dropping to his knees.

The Merchant saw that Weakness didn't have the same intimidating air around him. All that could be seen on his face was pure exhaustion. Taking advantage of the moment, The Merchant finally regained his confidence and swagger. He ordered the guards to surround Weakness.

Weakness stood still, letting every moment pass as an opportunity to gain as much energy as possible. Surrounded, Weakness didn't show a care in the world. He slowly and deeply breathed in and out.

The Merchant and Lü Zhi were practically beside themselves, knowing that information was the most important part of fighting, negotiating, and life itself. They felt naked and blind dealing with a foe they didn't know.

While racking their brains, Lü Zhi finally came up with something and said, "Weakness, surrender yourself and Daisuke or face the consequences."

Weakness looked at her and asked in a heavy tone, "Oh, what consequences?"

With his one eye fixed on her, Lü Zhi was startled at the intensity coming from his body

again. She said, "You and your little friend might be able to get away today, but what about all those slaves? Will you be able to live with the guilt of abandoning them to a painful, horrifying death?"

Chapter Seven

My Declaration of War

Weakness had a surprised look on his face for a moment, but then he started laughing hysterically as if he had just heard the funniest joke of all time. The Merchant thought threatening all the slaves was a good way to deal with Weakness and get him to stop killing in the first place, but once he heard his opponent's laughter, he had a bad premonition. At first, Weakness was looking Lü Zhi in the eyes, but after he finished laughing, he turned his gaze to the top of the wall leading to the outer part of the city. Then, he disappeared again.

Lü Zhi noticed where his gaze was before he disappeared, so she turned in that direction. Moments later, Weakness reappeared.

Weakness called out to the crowd, "The life of a slave is a fate worse than death. Do you think there was even a chance

I was going to take you up on that offer? Let me show you my answer to your question, Lü Zhi."

Then, he let his black weapon disappear and raised his hand above his head. High above in the sky, a tiny black-violet dot appeared. It was so small that those in the crowd couldn't see it. As more time passed, the dot began to get bigger. The bigger the dot grew, the more powerful it became.

Once it grew to be the size of a building, a powerful suction force started to manifest, causing the dot to float down and get closer to the slave town. Slowly, buildings and land started to rise into the sky and disappear behind the black-violet substance. As it grew, the dot started to suck up the slaves too. Screams could be heard first at the edge of the city, as anything that didn't have The Merchant's tier-two mid-level protection formation or above disappeared into the sky.

The people around The Merchant and Lü Zhi were shocked by the absurd scene in front of them. It was like a black sky had appeared out of nowhere. Lü Zhi's mouth was wide open, and her eyes shook out of fear when Weakness displayed his ability. She thought he had a rare teleportation ability, but after seeing the scene in front of her, she knew she couldn't be more wrong.

The Merchant was in a similar situation. What he saw made him think that the end of days had arrived, and he felt utterly powerless because he had no idea what to do. He panicked and shouted for everyone to aim at Weakness and kill him with nothing but fear of the unknown to drive them. Every source user working under The Merchant in the city who could hear his voice and had their long-range weapons sent a barrage of attacks to where Weakness was standing. However, the closer those attacks got to Weakness, the more force was applied to them. Pretty soon, everyone without protection was sucked into the sky.

The whole slave town was covered overhead by the black-violet substance, and there wasn't a single slave, shack, structure, or foundation to be seen. After all the slave town and most of the outer part of the city was gone, Weakness put his hand down, causing the black-violet substance to shrink until it was completely gone.

Weakness looked over to The Merchant and said, "Nothing in this life will ever hold me down again. I declare that, underneath the sun, only one of us will live. I won't allow something like you to draw breath for much longer."

He turned to Lü Zhi. Instantly, a chilling glare appeared in Weakness's eye. He said, "While I may show mercy to most of these scum by killing them, I promise you that the gift of death won't come easily to you because I will slowly and painfully pull you apart piece by piece over and over again until you beg for death. And even after that, it won't come."

Lü Zhi had lived most of her life in princess-level luxury in a corrupt tier-four country. The first time she could recall seeing a slave getting killed was when she was two years old. Her father and mother showed her that a slave's life didn't matter because they could always get more slaves by forced breeding, kidnapping, war, debt, prison, and even student loans if the owner received higher education they couldn't afford.

From then on, Lü Zhi learned that free labor was the greatest resource of her country's entire economy, even though being tier-four meant they had to have a certain level of education to pass the standards of the country's alliance. Because the country funded the corrupt members of the alliance, no one was sanctioned to act and stop the enslavement that was occurring. Maybe it was her upbringing or simply a different view of life that she had. Still, Lü Zhi enjoyed the feeling of elitism that being royalty in the country and possibly becoming its empress one day brought. She saw slaves as a never-ending resource that she could play with any way she saw fit.

Lü Zhi's parents went so far as to show her that she could kill one parent if a slave had a child. If the slave couple had two children, she could kill both parents to avoid suffering any loss in the long run. That's why, after killing a mother in front of her family that used to be four, guards restrained the father by pulling him away from his eldest son and his youngest daughter. In his native language, the man screamed out a message to each of his children.

Lü Zhi was handed a dagger and shown all the vital spots of the human body. Without hesitation, she quickly made work of him. The guards let the man's corpse drop to the ground, then Lü Zhi looked at his children and watched the daughter turn her head away and cry in the arms of her brother. Lü Zhi loved this scene because it enforced her belief that cruelty would keep the slave's head down in fear, hoping not to be picked when someone else is selected to be used like a consumable. However, to her surprise, she saw a different look in the eyes of the slave's son, but she didn't understand what it was.

It wasn't until years later when she saw her parents brutally murdered and their corpses paraded through the streets while her country was overthrown that she understood the look in that boy's eyes that day. His hatred was the purest form of hatred that existed. It didn't fade with time. It only got stronger because it caused a toxic flame to burn inside a person, and the only way to get rid of any of those feelings was to inflict as much destruction on the target of that fury.

That boy destroyed the whole Lü regime and publicly executed almost all the leader's family, the higher-ups in the government, their families, and all enslavers within three generations. Lü Zhi only got out alive because she smuggled herself out of the country in a slave transport, which was how she met Robert.

When Lü Zhi saw the same look in Weakness's eye, she had a premonition of losing everything she had once again, so she screamed at the top of her lungs and frantically threw her dagger at his head. The weapon got some distance, but it was not enough to do anything to Weakness practical. The Merchant boosted the dagger with his level three source manipulation, and without warning, the dagger was inches away from Weakness's head. Caught off guard, Weakness shifted away at the last moment and inwardly cursed. He thought, *Damn it, I revealed one of my trump cards that I was gonna show the next time we fought.*

Before, Weakness left hints that the way his teleportation worked was that he had to see where he was teleporting to. By moving away from the dagger, he showed his ability to teleport reflexively and shift a few feet away from his previous location. Since he used such a move, he spent way more energy than expected and found himself tired. Weakness was decisive, so he teleported out of the area. Before, he never showed that he could teleport outside his eyesight because he wanted to buy as much time as possible for this moment.

Once Weakness was nowhere to be seen, The Merchant began ordering guards to check around the city for any traces of where Weakness could have gone. Lü Zhi pointed out that she saw that Weakness would look where he would appear next, so they assumed that he was still in the city.

Twenty minutes later, miles away from the city, Weakness appeared on one of the routes back to the wasteland. He was drenched in sweat and unable to control his breathing. "Fucking shit! I can't keep this up much longer."

While The Merchant and all his minions thought that Weakness was unfathomable and close to unbeatable, it couldn't be further from the truth. Weakness forcibly used a large amount of foreign source energy to empower his spirit and body within a concise amount of time. Due to the massive strain this left on him, he broke every bone, muscle, and nerve in his body with each movement, tearing apart his spirit repeatedly while forcing his body to heal and strengthen again and again. While his body wasn't as skinny as before, he didn't consume any nourishment, so it was like using sand to build a castle. Once a strong enough breeze blew, it would bring everything toppling down.

Now that he was far enough away to ensure no one could follow him, Weakness collapsed. "Don't have any more time," said Weakness as a hand-sized black-violet circle appeared in his hand.

A bandaged and unconscious Daisuke was sucked out of the circle. "All these years, I only counted on myself. Who would have known that I had to rely on someone at the time of my victory?"

Weakness put his hand on Daisuke's chest and let the black-violet energy sink into his body to heal him through both old and new wounds while also removing the bandages from his

body. With each second that passed, Daisuke's complexion grew healthier while Weakness's only got worse. By the time he was done healing Daisuke, Weakness lost consciousness.

Moments later, Daisuke slowly opened his eyes. At first, he wasn't sure what was going on, but as he traced his memories, all the painful truths came to the surface. Daisuke could only clinch his fists hard enough to draw blood to keep himself from shedding a single tear. After letting his brain push the negative thoughts into the corner of his mind, he sat up and noticed that his best friend had collapsed beside him with his hand on Daisuke's chest.

Nothing made sense. The last thing Daisuke remembered was The Merchant's hand moving toward his head while he was severely injured, but he woke up in another location with Weakness. He felt better than ever as the power he felt earlier was more stable, and he knew that he was now a tier-three way of the body source user. After looking at his surroundings, Daisuke recognized the familiar path and trees in the area and decided on his next move.

"The secret village for freed slaves has been compromised, so I need to get there as soon as possible to figure out what to do next. But Weakness doesn't look like he will last long enough to get there. I'll change my initial plan and go to our secret allies at the Winter Herb Village. Weakness doesn't look good, and they are the only people we can turn to when it comes to injuries."

Daisuke was confident that he could turn to the Winter Herb clan because they were one of the few secrets he had kept from Lü Zhi. Daisuke had saved the village leader's daughter from being killed by beasts two years before, so he felt he could trust them because they seemed like they repaid kindness with kindness.

Daisuke looked at Weakness and realized that, after so many years in bondage, he had never once called Weakness by any other name. "No longer will I allow anyone to call you by your slave name of 'Weakness.' From now on, I will call you 'Pride' because when I think back on our bond, I can only feel pride."

After quickly formulating a plan, Daisuke ripped off his clothing and tied Pride to his back. He was glad that he had filled Pride's stomach with as much food as possible earlier because he wouldn't have to worry about either of them starving in the next few days. He was concerned about Pride being unable to stand the temperature from the snow now that it was reaching the coldest temperature during the season of Evil Frost, so he circulated source energy throughout his body to raise both of their body temperatures. With a firm plan in place and all his negative thoughts pushed down to the corner of his mind, Daisuke moved forward with newfound resolve.

Chapter Eight

The Winter Herb Clan

Kneeling in the private garden of the Winter Herb clan's patriarch, a lovely young woman tended to the most vibrant plants. In her simple white robe with sky-blue outlines and designs, she almost faded into the background of the snow all around her. While most people would have been inside their homes due to the massive drop in temperature during the season of Evil Frost, there were a few individuals born with a special constitution that allowed them to not be affected by the deep cold. She was one of those people, and due to her position as the patriarch's youngest daughter and unique constitution, she was second to none in the village.

Her clan members treated her as a holy woman, a spokesman for Evil Frost. To go against her, in their eyes, was to go against nature. Due to this belief her people had about her, she had always practically been alone ever since she was born. While her father doted on her as a child, her elder sisters and brothers couldn't stand the sight of her. When the young girl was born, the cold from her body was so extreme that her mother nearly died. Her mother's health was severely damaged for the rest of her days after giving birth.

It wasn't until her mother had another child, five years later, that the woman lost her strength to survive childbirth. The young girl's mother died midway through birthing the girl's younger sibling. Since then, the girl and her younger brother were viewed by the rest of their siblings as being cancerous.

She had to grow up quickly in such a harsh environment, so she became an extremely knowledgeable herbalist by reading all of the clan's books and scrolls about botany. While she had all the knowledge, she couldn't put it to good use outside of tending to the herbs in the garden. With her body temperature so low, she couldn't use spirit fire to create pills because no one could produce a fire hot enough to not be snuffed out by her coldness.

Each day was as tiring as the last, and she wanted nothing more than to fade away and escape from her life of endless isolation and pain. But she couldn't give in to those thoughts because there was still someone who needed her in life. This person was her sun and stars, one of the only things to bring color and meaning into her life—her younger brother.

While she understood that her siblings hated her because they would never be able to experience the warmth of love from their mother again after she passed, her little brother wasn't as lucky. All he heard was how he took the person they loved most. With no real power or influence to stop her siblings' cruelty, all she could do was try to replace her mother for her little brother in his life. She sang the songs her mother used to sing to her as a baby. She learned to prepare meals exactly like her mother used to, but she had to have someone else cook them

since the fire wouldn't burn near her. She even learned how to knit and sew by watching others so that she could make all the clothes her little brother would need.

As time went on, her younger brother, Yukidori, grew into a bright young boy surrounded by friends. He never once felt like he was lacking anything in this life. With all the love Yukiko gave him, Yukidori truly hated the rest of his family. He hated his other siblings for treating his sister so terribly. He never cared for his father because his absence in their lives allowed the older siblings to commit such cruelty to Yukiko. It helped that only he and his sister had pure white hair in their family, so when his other siblings verbally insulted him, he didn't care. The only thing that got to him was how much it hurt his sister while she tried to hide the pain from him.

After trimming the plants and herbs, Yukiko stood up and took the ones that were ready into the tier-two pill master's hut near the village gate. She left them to be prepared by the clan's chief of medicine. On the way to and from there, people moved out of her way and gave a slight bow of their heads toward her. After many years, Yukiko became completely numb to these actions and didn't react to them anymore. Once she was a few yards away from the main gate, she heard a commotion from the guards stationed there. As more people crowded the gate, a large figure could be seen slowly moving toward them, coming from outside the village's environment control formation.

*****

With their spirit source weapons up, ten guards made out what looked like a giant of a man carrying something on his back. After a few minutes, the man reached a dozen yards from the gate, but the guards called out to him in the language of the Central Plains, "Stop right there!"

However, the man continued to move toward them as if he hadn't heard their command. He didn't even raise his feet to walk. He just slid across the ground. Seeing that their words had fallen on deaf ears, the guards began to condense their source energy into their weapons as fire, water, or ice appeared on the edges of their weapons. They were preparing to attack, but a voice yelled for them to stop. The guards turned around to see Yukiko drop her basket and run toward the intruder.

The crowd parted the way, fearing being frozen by Yukiko's touch. Even the guards weren't brave enough to block her path, as they saw her as a natural disaster. But Yukiko didn't care because she recognized the giant of a man. He was once the boy who had saved her years ago in the Ice Forest. Although he was much taller, his skin was as flawless as jade and almost as pale as her skin.

Many emotions came bubbling up to the surface as Yukiko recalled that wonderful month when he stayed at the village with them. For the first time in a long time, she was able to talk to someone besides her younger brother without being on guard for things to get bad like they usually did. When she finally got next to him, she noticed a brown-skinned young man with skinny limbs and a damaged body tied to Daisuke's back. She put her hands on Daisuke, and his focus returned.

During his journey, he had only hunted a few small animals to feed Pride and used his source energy to keep his best friend from freezing due to Evil Frost or dying from the massive wounds plaguing his body. After finally noticing that he had made it to the Winter Herb clan's non-combatant village, he looked at Yukiko and gave her a smile that blew away all her negative emotions accumulated over the last two years. Having found that he had made it to his goal, Daisuke collapsed face forward into the snow.

Yukiko started screaming Daisuke's name to get him to wake up, but he wouldn't move an inch. She ordered the guards to carry Daisuke and his companion to her hut. No matter how much the guards didn't want to let outsiders into the village, no one was brave enough to go against the holy woman. Two guards tried and failed to lift Daisuke, so two more came and all four of them struggled to carry him. Another guard untied Pride from Daisuke's back and easily carried him in both arms to the hut.

Several hours later, the village's main healer walked out of Yukiko's hut to greet her. After seeing Daisuke again, Yukiko's usual temperament of avoidance and quietness was replaced with the confidence of a leader who had to command others.

Yukiko asked, "How are they?"

The healer said, "The large man is currently doing fine. It seems like he was exhausted and famished. From what I can tell, he has constantly been moving without rest for at least a week now. If he had been by himself, he wouldn't look this bad, but when examining the brown- skinned man, I found massive traces of the large man's source energy coursing through his body, protecting his vital organs, keeping his bones in place, and creating a thin membrane above his skin to protect him from Evil Frost". As the healer said this, a slight smile formed across her face as she thought of how far someone would go for another person. But that smile quickly faded and was replaced with a look of horror when she thought about her other patient.

"The brown-skinned man, however, is in some of the worst shape I have ever seen. Most of his bones are broken, and his muscles torn beyond belief. He is malnourished to the point that he has the body of a fourteen-year-old boy, but he is clearly at least sixteen years old. The worst of it is that none of his old wounds were ever able to heal properly. The fact that he is alive is honestly amazing."

Yukiko shuttered at the details. While she only knew a little about the man with Daisuke, there was only one type of person whose situation was ever this bad: an enslaved person on an extremely cruel enslaver's property.

Yukiko asked, "When will they both wake up?"

The healer replied, "The large man will gain consciousness by tomorrow morning. I gave him a mid-level tier-two recovery pill, and he had been previously soaking in a potent herbal bath.

Most of his source energy will recover overnight, so he will be starving in the morning. However, the brown-skinned man is another story. The fact that he is alive is already a miracle, so only one thing can keep him going once the large man's source energy dries up and stops protecting him."

"What is it?" asked Yukiko.

The healer said, "He will need to take the peak level tier-two rebirth pill and survive the unbelievable pain of having his body turning inside out while melting and breaking over and over again for at least thirty-six hours."

The more Yukiko heard, the worse she felt. She couldn't say she knew Daisuke well, as he had only been with them for a very short month. But whenever she asked about his life, Daisuke would always somehow bring up Pride, the person he considered a brother and best friend. While she wished he had talked more about himself than his best friend, Yukiko also felt closer to him because they were similar in how their eyes visibly brightened up when they talked about someone they loved. She couldn't imagine how she would give this terrible news to him when he woke up, but she decided not to stand still.

Yukiko said to the healer, "Search our libraries and old scrolls. I want the recipe for the rebirth pill and all its ingredients as soon as possible. I won't take anything less as an excuse."

"Yes, miss," said the healer, rushing away from Yukiko's hut. Yukiko walked into her hut and saw the two unconscious young men resting.

Yukiko knelt down next to Daisuke and Pride, pondering how she could help the weaker man. Out of anyone in the village, she had one of the highest level of source ability at the peak of mid-level tier-two as far as she knew.

While thinking about what to do, a black figure began to materialize out of thin air near the door. Yukiko turned around but couldn't make out its silhouette because all the lights went out as if even heaven's light was too scared to get near the figure. When Yukiko saw it was a person, she jumped up and stood in fear, keeping herself between the monster in front of her and the unconscious young men behind her.

The figure had no physical features where its face should have been, which made it all the more terrifying, but its presence showed no hostility. Yukiko's brain was spinning, trying to figure out what was going on. She felt frozen until the creature started moving toward Daisuke. At that moment, a chilling anger arose inside Yukiko. Without thinking, she attacked the creature. This was the first time in her life that she'd attacked another creature.

She created a frost wave so thin and sharp that anything with a physical body beneath the peak level tier two would be cut in half and shattered by frostbite. When it hit the mysterious figure, it split the figure in half as the frost wave traveled toward the hut's wall and dissipated before causing damage to the surroundings.

For a moment, Yukiko was overcome by a feeling of sorrow as she thought back to how she caused her mother to die all those years before. Her simple existence caused death to appear around her once again, and the pain inside caused her to lose focus on the being she thought she had killed. The two halves of the black figure stitched themselves back together and extended pieces of themselves toward Yukiko, Daisuke, and Pride.

Once in contact with the figure, Yukiko found herself in a completely black area filled with smokey shadows and a black light that illuminated the place. All she could see was an endless expanse of pure darkness. Once there, a part of the floor started to grow taller, then a man covered in a black shroud appeared before her.

Looking at Yukiko, he said, "Welcome, Child of Nature."

Chapter Nine

Power is Gained Through Suffering

Yukiko couldn't make sense of her whole day. From her mind-numbing routine of taking care of her clan's most dangerous herbs to the shocking reunion she had with Daisuke and the feeling of helplessness she felt once she found out that Pride was going to die without receiving his special treatment, none of her emotions compared to the bewilderment she was feeling. She stood in a void full of darkness and silence that she didn't think could exist. In front of her was a dark figure with the silhouette of a six-foot-two lean and muscular man. His voice was hollow and reverberated throughout the whole space.

Yukiko stood in one place in fear. She didn't know where she was or how to leave. After a few moments, she realized she couldn't find Daisuke or Pride. With her mind racing, the dark figure snapped what appeared to be a finger, then a loud sound exploded outward, knocking Yukiko on her rear.

After getting her attention, the figure moved slightly closer to Yukiko and said, "Child of Nature, it is rude to not answer when someone is talking to you."

The arrogance and pride mixed in the figure's voice sounded unpleasant to the ears. Yukiko finally calmed down, stood back up, and said, "Who are you? Where are we? Where are Daisuke and Pride?"

The dark figure smirked at Yukiko and turned its hand upside down. With that action, the darkness receded, and in its place appeared a study room covered in the finest silks and linens with a tacky look of gold plating almost covering the entire space. There was furniture made from extravagant materials like agarwood and foreign designs of statues and paintings clearly looted from many different places. The figure sat on one side of two chairs that were facing each other with a knee-high table in between and gestured for Yukiko to sit in the other chair.

With no other option, Yukiko sat down and focused on calming her breathing. The dark figure tapped its index finger on the table, and out of the table appeared two cups made of shiny gold-polished porcelain filled with a black substance. The black figure took a sip of the beverage and smiled, then gestured his hands to invite Yukiko to drink. He told her to take the medicine if she wanted answers to her questions.

Yukiko sat across from her mysterious kidnapper, contemplating whether to drink the questionable substance in front of her. Quickly, she realized that if he had wanted to harm her, he wouldn't have gone about it in such a roundabout way. She put the drink to her lips and drank it in one gulp. As soon as it touched her tongue, Yukiko tasted the wild rabbit stew her mother used to make. Her mind went back to the memories she shared with her mother. She began to cry tears of anguish for what felt like hours until she felt the liquid pour down into her stomach. Its substance quickly spread throughout her body. At first, it was a slow and painful process, like small pieces of her body and spirit exploding and repeatedly imploding while they grew repeatedly. Finally, after five horrifying minutes of barely holding her mind, body, and spirit together with just her tenacity, all that was left were her bones, muscles, and limbs to slowly fracture, grow, and strengthen as much as they could while she got used to the pain.

Being a spirit user, Yukiko's body was way less powerful compared to her spirit, so she was helpless against an opponent who was physically stronger and could get in close range to tag her with a hit. But whatever was in the black substance restructured and optimized both her body and spirit. Without experiencing a single moment of body source cultivation ever in her life, her body had reached tier-two primary levels in physical capabilities, and her spirit source energy level shot through the roof. She went from tier-two mid-peak straight to tier-two peak.

After a transformation that could only be described as severe torture at best to any bystander, Yukiko was simply relieved to not experience the pain anymore. She started to notice the changes she had gone through. Her whole life, she could only remember the world feeling numb to her sense of touch due to her cold skin. But after drinking the substance, her pale white skin gained a lot of color, and her complexion reminded Yukiko of her late mother's. Most importantly, she could feel more than the cold. For the first time, Yukiko wept tears that didn't instantly freeze to her face, giving her another reason to cry.

While trying and failing to calm herself down, the black figure watched Yukiko's transformation process with a book in his hands, writing down his observations as if she was an experiment. Seeing this, Yukiko focused on her dissatisfaction with him and pulled herself together.

She looked at him and said, "I did what you told me to do. Now it's time for you to give me some answers. Where are my friends? Explain why I am here!"

The black figure let go of the book, and it floated in the air while the writing tool he was using continued to take notes. He gave Yukiko a quick nod, then changed the environment again so that they were transported to what looked like an all-white medical room with Daisuke and Pride sleeping in beds.

Yukiko unclenched a few of her nerves, finally no longer fearing the worst, but she remained vigilant to find out what was going on. She went and stood beside her unconscious friends so that they would not get split up again. Then, she waited for the black figure to begin talking because she was already tired from the day's events. She was in no mood to let anything else physically, mentally, or psychologically scarring occur again.

"I see you are quick to change methods of interaction when dealing with a situation you have little to no control over to find the one that leads to the optimal result. Smart move, Child. I like learning more about you with every passing moment," said the black figure.

For Yukiko, hearing her thought process spelled out plainly like that was unpleasant. But letting him bait her into reacting to such childish provocation was not something she was willing to do.

She focused on her breathing again. With that action, she noticed a new sensation connecting her spirit and body. It felt like the call of a bottomless dark existence, and with her concentrating on it, the bottomless dark existence noticed her and looked back. The moment of connection sent shivers down her spine, and she broke it as soon as she established it and was back in the white room.

The black figure, sitting in the room with her, saw the potential Yukiko had displayed through his short test and finally decided to drop the façade he had until now. "Enough games."

The black figure's demeanor changed with those two words going from an annoyingly arrogant trickster to an unfathomable entity. Yukiko got up and took a step back just before he continued to speak.

"I apologize for the show up until now. Still, I have to be careful with whom I interact with due to the consequences that could appear."

The black figure's shadowy aura was sucked into his body, and his appearance became clear. He wore a simple undershirt and a detailed outer robe with a multitude of beasts chasing each other with a black full-face mystic beast mask. Gone was the sense of being unfathomable. He no longer had a sense of presence. If she wasn't looking at him, Yukiko would have sworn that she was alone in a white room with her two unconscious friends.

"Enough of all these games, deception, and misdirection. What do you want from me?

Why am I here?" she said with anger in her voice.

"In the spirit of being straightforward, what I want from you is to create an alliance for the foreseeable future. Without someone to help me coordinate treatment, the boy you call Pride will die, and Daisuke might never recover from the grief of losing him."

Yukiko threw away her indignation and focused. "What do I need to do? How can I trust what you are telling me?"

"I'll need every book and scroll you can get your hands on, especially the list of the ingredients you need for the rebirth pill you were discussing earlier outside the hut. I'll also need people with skills and training in various jobs. You can trust me because we both want those two to be okay, so we have no reason not to collaborate."

As Yukiko examined her interaction with the black figure, she was stuck between preparing for the worst, thinking this was some trick to destroy them all, and choosing to believe he was telling the truth. With nothing to push her in either direction, she chose to believe him. "Until proven otherwise, I'll trust you for now. I can get you everything you've asked for, but what do you need my people for? I won't sacrifice any of them."

The black figure extended his hand toward her but stopped in the space between them. "No one has to die. I just need them to do their usual work in a location of my choosing while wearing this special pin," he said while reaching his free hand into his outer robe to retrieve a dark pin made from an unknown substance. "After some time, I will be done. Pride and I will leave so you and Daisuke can do whatever you want."

"Why are you taking Pride with you? You seem too powerful to care or need people like us," she said, not reacting to the hand extended to her. She was completely unaware of the meaning of his gesture.

"Just because we are working together doesn't mean I'm going to reveal anything more than I am willing to. Let's be honest with each other here. You don't care about this damaged person. You only care about him because you love Daisuke, so you translate part of those feelings to those he cares about." The black figure withdrew his hand, and in a waving motion, his hand moved Yukiko and Daisuke back to Yukiko's hut. "I'll do my part and keep Pride alive so call my name when you have what I need."

"But I don't know your name," she said. Yukiko was once again filled with anger. She was frustrated about practically being ordered around by some powerful stranger who not only invaded her clan but even her own home. She was angry because what he said about her feelings for Daisuke was true, including that she didn't really care so much about Pride.

"For now, just call me E." All trace of the man faded away with the sound of his voice.

Walking out of the hut, Yukiko headed toward the village's underground storage warehouse to get the supplies.

As soon as Yukiko left the room, Daisuke slowly opened his eyes and sat upright on his bed. He silently contemplated all the information he had heard. Less than a minute later, a dark film appeared in the middle of the air, and like opening a large door, E reappeared.

"I know you have questions and have no reason to trust me. But believe me when I say I have no malicious schemes against any of you. If you want to have a conversation, just follow me."

Without hesitation, Daisuke walked through the film and disappeared from Yukiko's

room.

Chapter Ten
Plans For The Future

The next morning the Sun rose, blanketing the hidden valley where the Winter Herb clan lived in a heavenly glow. But there was no warmth felt from the Sun. Sitting at the highest peak was a ruined temple where only members of the main Miya family were allowed access. Only when it was the season of Evil Frost was Yukiko able to cultivate because she needed the climate to be cold enough to absorb the abundant frost element in the environment. But today was different. After going to every spot in the village to try out cultivating, she reached a conclusion: whatever it was that E did to her the day before had changed her life.

Last night, for the first time, she made a meal with her own hands for herself and her younger brother. While it wasn't perfect, it was the best meal she had ever had because she tasted warmth for the first time.

Yukiko's body and spirit were ever cultivating in her sleep, and it didn't stop when she woke up. As long as she wasn't doing anything strenuous, it felt like she was cultivating without even trying. After seeing no problems, she used her new body's capabilities to quickly make her way back to her hut since she had stayed at her younger brother's hut the night before.

Walking into her hut, she felt a pulsating feeling throughout her body. It felt like all her muscles were frozen, but she couldn't understand why it was happening until she saw Daisuke meditating on his bed. He was cultivating a new way of the body mantra called the Great Body Forging Technique. Previously, he used an incomplete mantra, but E gave him a new body cultivation mantra the day before. The difference between the two cultivation techniques was like night and day.

Yukiko's body unconsciously froze because a body that didn't use a cultivation method couldn't hope to compare in the same realm to someone who used a cultivation method unless they were a heaven-defying existence. Momentarily shocked, Yukiko sat beside Daisuke and silently stared at him, enjoying the view.

After a few minutes, Daisuke stopped cultivating and opened his eyes to see Yukiko watching him with a slight smile on her face. Since he arrived, he hadn't gotten a chance to appreciate how beautiful Yukiko had become. She was no longer the tiny, frightened teen he had met two years ago while hunting. She was like a princess of nature who seemed so close yet so far. Daisuke felt his ears becoming hotter, but as soon as the warm feeling entered his heart, it only reminded him of Min. It felt like a knife—that feeling only brought up what he had been suppressing in the back of his mind—and cut him deep emotionally all over again.

Yukiko could see the pain in his eyes and was saddened. She didn't know what was bothering him, but she wanted to help him no matter what.

Daisuke broke the silence between them and jokingly said, "It has been so long that I almost forgot how to get back here."

Yukiko decided not to try and dig up information. She played along. "Wow, two years of not seeing each other, and here you are with no gifts. But clearly, trouble is following you. Am I right?"

"Hahaha, no longer the wide-eyed girl who was astonished no matter what I said or did, I
see."

They continued with their friendly banter for a few more minutes before Yukiko finally
addressed what they had been talking around. "Okay, enough games. What is going on?"

Daisuke stopped smiling and slowly explained everything that had happened. He told Yukiko about him getting the previous mantra that shaped his body to look like a young god to meeting and falling in love with Min. He also told her about Min's betrayal that led to him almost dying at the hands of The Merchant. After twenty minutes of pouring his heart out, without realizing it, Yukiko had moved closer to him and was holding his hand. At that moment, Daisuke felt his heart lighten. All he could think of was wanting to stay in the moment.

Without warning, the black film reappeared and interrupted their tender moment.

Daisuke and Yukiko found themselves back in the hospital room. Pride was still in bed, unconscious, while Daisuke and Yukiko were standing over him. Only Daisuke was shocked because of how stealthy the movements were because Yukiko had grown up in the small wasteland and from yesterday's experience she had grown used to the unexpected.

In this place, most cultivators wouldn't go unless the environment was highly effective for their cultivation, so there weren't many ways for her to see how big the world was. She was not shocked because she didn't understand how difficult what E had done was. Daisuke had no idea how Pride had found himself a hidden master with amazing skills or abilities to hide himself from society.

Everything finally made sense. Daisuke realized how Pride was able to murmur the body cultivation technique to him all those years ago. He knew how he and Pride were able to escape the City of Noel together. With this realization, Daisuke knelt and bowed his head in total admiration and respect for his friend's savior.

"One kind word can warm three winter months, but your kind action has warmed three lifetimes. I swear that this debt will be paid within my lifetime," Daisuke uttered with his eyes fixed on the ground.

E reacted as if being thanked so seriously was annoying and waved his hand in a shooing motion to signal for Daisuke to stop. "I have given you enough time to talk with each other, so let's move on and discuss what has to be done. Yesterday, after you left, Yukiko, I had a short conversation with Daisuke. We made a similar arrangement between the two of us like the one I have with you. So, if things work the way I plan, I shall be gone from here within the month with my . . . partner."

Daisuke was saddened. His plan for what to do after getting away from The Merchant was never truly set in stone. He had just worked toward being free, but even then, he never had full faith in himself to be able to make it. Now, after no longer being held captive, he felt both a heavy weight lift off his shoulders and a profound emptiness that came with accomplishing one of his main goals. With no path in front of himself, Daisuke felt lost and without purpose. All those years of tireless training, endless beatings as a slave for the city's guards, and deadly trips in search of the wastelands felt like they had been for nothing. In the end, if it weren't for someone else, he would be dead or worse.

At the lowest point in his mind, Daisuke saw the corpses of all the people he had had the power to save over the years but forced himself not to out of fear that his heroics would give him away and get him killed before he could do execute his ultimate plan. Hundreds of bodies were scattered around him with a pool of blood underneath his feet. Slowly, the tide rose, attempting to wash him away.

But Daisuke felt a strength that calmed his mind and radiated from his hand. It came from the very hand that Yukiko was holding. Yukiko's very presence was a light that Daisuke found could keep the dark thoughts from creeping into his mind. He couldn't understand what he was feeling, but he knew that he had never felt anything like it before.

E had finally had enough of the display of emotions and powered through. "I will keep it short so that we can move forward. The first issue is that, since we have escaped from the city, it

is only a matter of time before The Merchant sends a request out for a slave hunter if he can't find us on his own."

Yukiko's face gasped in horror while Daisuke steeled his resolve. There wasn't a single person who hadn't heard of the slave hunters. These vicious beasts usually caused despair in those who were on the receiving end of their missions. For the slaves, being tracked and caught by a slave hunter meant dying a cruel death. The slave hunter usually destroyed everything in the area of their prey to set an example for others to never think about harboring a runaway slave. For those like The Merchant, who utilized slaves, there was nothing but pride in getting to see slave hunters at work because almost every little boy from such a society who sanctioned slavery dreamt of growing up and punishing the slaves for not knowing their place and returning the property to its rightful owner.

Until this point, Yukiko was able to calmly listen and take in as much information as possible, but being told that a mass murderer was looking for them was too much to bear. She had lived her whole life in the village, and while she couldn't be close to anyone except her younger brother, she still cared for all her people. She went from helping her crush to casting potential doom on her entire clan.

"How can you be so sure that a slave hunter will be coming after all of you?" Yukiko asked with slight panic in each word she spoke. She let go of Daisuke's hand without realizing it.

E opened his hand, and above it, a dark substance converged to form a screen that captured the image of E partially possessing Pride's body to stab The Merchant in the back. But to anyone who saw what happened, it looked like Pride did the stabbing.

"If we had succeeded, The Merchant would have died, which would have shut down the city's formation and left it in an extremely vulnerable position. There would be a succession conflict as well, so no one would be able to make the final decision on multiple problems. They would first have to get a tier-four/city-level formation user to rebuild the destroyed formation just to make sure they don't freeze over during the next six months of Evil Frost. With that gigantic money-consuming project, it would take them a long time to complete, leaving no money to contact the slaver's union to hire the slave hunter. However, The Merchant is alive and vengeful after almost losing his spirit core, especially to a sneak attack by a foreigner slave. I wouldn't be surprised if he's already placed a bounty on both of your heads."

After digesting all this, Daisuke felt guilty for dragging Yukiko and her clan into his mess. Once he woke up and saw how broken Pride was, he stopped his original plan of going to the hidden village because he didn't believe that Pride would be able to survive long enough to get there. Even if his best friend made it to the village, there was no one with the skills to heal him.

Daisuke looked Yukiko in the eyes and struggled to find the right words to express how sorry he was. But he didn't see blame in her eyes. Daisuke saw her inner strength. It was as if he had truly seen her for the first time. Then, he grabbed Yukiko's hand and tried to show his support.

"No matter who shows up, I'll be here with you to defend you and your people to repay this kindness."

E shot the idea down as soon as it was spoken. "No, that will just lead to everyone dying after you defend the village three or four times at best. You may repel them the first two times because they will likely underestimate what you can do, but they will learn their lesson and outnumber you. The only reason you were able to take on an entire city by yourself was because the lower soldiers had no idea how to fight a way of the body user because the higher-

ups didn't let them know what was going on before you got to the middle layer of the city. If their higher-ups had clued them in about you, you would have been captured much sooner. Now that you both know how serious the situation is, I believe you won't have any issues following my orders if you all want to live."

Yukiko and Daisuke nodded in agreement.

"All right, here is the plan." E began to lay out the tasks needed to be done if they hoped to survive.

Chapter Eleven

Back in the City of Noel

Two weeks later, inside his private cultivation room, The Merchant began cultivating for the first time in decades. His halberd was hovering behind him, surrounded by a small tornado. His eyes were bloodshot, and a permanent glare was stuck on his face. For fourteen days, The Merchant had been silent and alone in this one room. Most of the time, he kept his eyes closed and replayed the biggest failure of his life. After the hundredth time, he became boiling mad. By the thousandth time, he was on the brink of insanity. And by the ten thousandth time, his face became cold like stone, but the anger was always visible.

After getting stabbed, he called over a third-tier healer from one of the many connections he had made over the decades after taking over the City of Noel. He even paid for the healer to use the teleportation tunnel to cut the travel time from two months to three days. After being healed, he was told to rest for four days and not use any source abilities. Even on those days of rest, The Merchant never relaxed because he always had the same question on his mind: How did he do it?

When he was younger, The Merchant traveled with his older brother and saw the entire State of Moon. He saw all the great sects and clans compete for the position of Head of State, and almost all of them fought with everything they had to make sure to win. Back then, The Merchant saw a butterfly crush a mountain, a quill split a lake in half, and a finger blot out a sun the size of a sea. All of them had massive fluctuations of energy coming off them. To this day, The Merchant still wakes up in the middle of the night sweating and dreaming of being on the receiving end of any of those attacks.

This time, it was different. There was no rise or fall in temperature, no shadow that blotted out the sun, and no violent shaking from the shockwave upon impact. The only evidence that the slave Weakness had attempted to take The Merchant's life was the bandage that covered his midsection. The Merchant had been debating with himself for two weeks because he had to make a tough decision.

As a trusted and respected slave merchant who had been in business for half a century, The Merchant knew how the game was played and how to protect what was his. One of the very first rules that enslavers pass down to their successors is to be in control at all times, no matter what happens. As long as a slave is involved in a matter, it becomes the enslaver's issue as well.

When the worst-case scenario occurs and a slave escapes from their enslaver, it becomes serious. Losing a slave is bad enough, but for the enslaver to not be able to find their slave with their available resources instantly brands the enslaver as incompetent trash.

While The Merchant's pride was screaming out to him to form a team of his most elite warriors and guards to track Weakness down as soon as possible, the strategic side of his brain kept listing issues he would encounter if he were to follow through on tracking Weakness down immediately. The more he thought about it, the more startled he was by Weakness's mind. The season of Evil Frost had just arrived, so there wasn't the possibility of moving in the open. Even if The Merchant were to go out and search for Weakness, he didn't believe he would be able to keep himself from freezing after using his source energy nonstop for five days. He would have even less time if he were to bring even one person with him. The energy consumption would turn the two of them into popsicles without them even realizing before it was too late.

As a formation user, The Merchant could make an environment isolation array like the one he maintained for the City of Noel. However, the cost of resources and time needed to set up even the smallest of strategic arrays would have heavily outweighed any possible gain. The more he thought about his problem, the more The Merchant saw that his skills and resources weren't suited for tracking down slaves in extreme environments.

His second option was to contact the Master's Union, a massive organization that was the authority on all things related to slaves. If he contacted them, they would send one of their slave hunters stationed in the State of Moon—someone extremely suited to the environment and with the skills needed to capture or kill a runaway slave. While this would have been the best solution to eliminate any threats, the Union would demote The Merchant from his current position. He would no longer oversee all slave trade in the wasteland for the State of Moon. As the best-case scenario, he would maintain the formations and arrays in the city while getting to keep his accumulated wealth.

At first, The Merchant was unwilling to even consider the second option, but when he thought back to who he would want to take over for him, the face of his secret son, Robert, flashed in his mind. Then, he started to give it a second thought. While in the middle of his thought, The Merchant heard a loud knock on the door into the room. When The Merchant opened the door, he saw that all his overseers had finally returned to the city, being led by Rod, Robert, and Lü Zhi.

"What is it?" he asked.

Everyone bowed to him, then Rod stepped forward while the others stepped back. "Sir, we have finished deciphering the map drawn by Daisuke showing their secret base and much more. After going over it, I see how I missed it. Daisuke and Weakness are hidden deep in the middle layer of the wastelands, nowhere near where we go hunting and exploring in the outer layer of the middle layer. The fact that they have some way of surviving out there year-round surrounded by those demonic beasts, spirit animals, savage clans, monsters, and the extreme cold that gets colder during Evil Frost without an environment isolation array is surprising. But if we can find out how they do it, we can take it for ourselves and take over the entire wasteland. All those natural resources would be ours."

The Merchant was slightly irritated by Rod, a subordinate who had been with him for two decades. While The Merchant had reached his peak abilities a long time ago, Rod was a natural cultivator at tier-three primary peak at the age of thirty. If it weren't for him secretly poisoning Rod all these years, Rod would have been tier-four by now. The jealousy

The Merchant felt for his follower led to him cuckolding him all those years ago. Whenever he was annoyed by Rod or felt that his subordinate had overstepped his bounds, The Merchant's petty mind drew comfort in the idea that a man that was his better in looks and potential was raising his bastard son.

"That would be a wise assessment if you hadn't realized the obvious. Robert, why is just following that map blind only going to lead to our collective doom?"

Robert felt conflicted when it came to The Merchant using his authority to put down his father publicly. Growing up, his father, Rod, treated every slight like air and always told him not to mind it, so Robert tried to do just that.

"If we look at it from the standpoint of our enemies, this was a plan with a backup plan. If we had acted like we didn't know what was going on and let them escape as the Immortal Slave wanted, we would have followed this map into who knows what that other slave Weakness would have had waiting for us. However, even now that we know what is going on, we can't help but still follow this map because it is our only clue to their whereabouts. The only things we can guarantee are the safe routes leading to their hidden village and the location of the village because Lü Zhi had the Immortal Slave draw this map himself. I believe that Weakness used the Immortal Slave as bait to attempt to kill you again, sir.

I thought slaves banded together, but this Weakness is cold, calculating, and especially cruel. We still haven't figured out what his capabilities are, but to be able to kill all those slaves with his black circle within seconds is horrifying for us. We can't use any hostages because he would sooner kill them than we would."

The Merchant was pleased by Robert's observation and found that paying for him to attend a prestigious school in the City of Plums was paying off. "Excellent! What would you recommend we do going forward?"

"I suggest we make teams of the way of the body users' slaves. Some of our most powerful spirit users can scout ahead to bring us information so we can then plot our supply

line, possibly ally or enslave some of the savage clans in the area, and plan our assault on the hidden village. Lü Zhi also had something to add regarding Weakness and his mysterious abilities."

"Lü Zhi, what do you have to say?"

Lü Zhi stepped forward and said, "When we were battling Weakness, several of us were focusing on his body movements and noticed some patterns. Whenever he teleported, he appeared right where his eye was pointing. The more he used his abilities, the sooner his body would slow down as if using his abilities put a huge strain on him. Also, whenever an attack struck him, he only protected his vitals while the rest of his body suffered the deep cuts."

The Merchant contemplated what his followers had brought to him and was pleased. "I know you are all hard at work keeping the City of Noel prosperous, so I trust every one of you to do what you do best. Robert, I am giving you another shot at proving yourself as an overseer.

Since you were the one who trained our group of body cultivator slaves, you will be in charge of them while Gil Eanes will be in charge of scouting.

Gil Eanes, a Portuguese man in his mid-forties, possessed a sun-kissed complexion, complemented by his brown eyes and hair, but his true essence was yet to be revealed. While he wore the standard uniform for all overseers made of tier-three cloth, he also wore a doublet with his family's spirit animal design over his heart.

"Scouting without being seen is what you pay me for. This job will turn out like all the rest: uneventful and boring," Gil Eanes said with a yawn.

The Merchant looked him in the eyes, and Gil Eanes immediately got the message to take what they were doing seriously. He straightened up to appease his boss.

"For now, we will operate as usual. I have already ordered a fresh new batch of slaves, so they will be here once Evil Frost is over. In place of powerless slaves, we will be using the tier-one guards and their families. Anyone who rebels will be killed on the spot to send a message to any others who want to resist. Now, move out."

For the rest of the day, screaming and crying could be heard for miles. If it wasn't for the blizzard outside the barrier, those who gave in had to bear the pain of the branding slave mark as it destroyed their bloodline. The bloodline, for many, was the only thing their family and this world gave them. Strengthening it every day with cultivation was a way of life for many people. The man who could create a plow with his source energy felt generations of his heritage slipping away before being gone forever.

The lucky slaves were able to maintain their sanity and resigned themselves to their fate, but the unfortunate ones became mad. Some lost their minds and attacked their enslavers, being killed a few seconds later because of their revolt. Others walked outside the barrier and froze within minutes of leaving the city, while their family members and friends held down the last of them to protect their lives as they were branded. For years to come, this day would be known as The Great Pain in the outer layer of the wastelands to all those in tier-one.

Chapter Twelve

The Hidden Village in The Fog

In the Winter Herb Village, Yukiko finished collecting all the ingredients needed to create Pride's rebirth pill, but things weren't looking great in her eyes. After researching and contacting the eight other clan allies throughout the middle layer of the wasteland, she found that the best success rate that any pill maker could tell her was around ten percent at best. This news was based on how difficult it was to produce pills during the season of Evil Frost when all fire elements were weakened if not snuffed out.

As she made her way to the edge of the village where they had set up a new hut for Pride and E, Yukiko felt the world shift around her before she got to climb the stairs to the door. Then, she found herself sitting in front of E in the same tacky golden room she met him during their first encounter. All the ingredients she had brought were gone.

"Don't worry, Yukiko, I'm preparing the ingredients as we speak. Tell me about your concerns. As partners, I believe we can clear up any issues as long as we don't pry into each other's business too much."

"How do you plan on finding someone skilled enough to refine that peak tier-two pill, especially in this weather? Everyone tells me that the success rate to make it once is too low for us to succeed with the amount we were able to acquire."

"We don't need anyone or anything else. Just leave it to be dealt with by me."

Yukiko would usually ask more questions but had learned her lesson to just let it go. "Then, I will leave you to it."

As she turned around, the black film split apart. She found herself standing at the bottom of the stairs, slightly sighing at the feeling of being forced to work for someone who didn't care for her presence or even to explain why he did what he did. She hoped to never be under the leadership of anyone like E again.

When she got to her hut, Yukiko started her new routine of cultivation. Now that she didn't have to cultivate under specific requirements, sitting on her bed, she visualized a white shrine gate being blanketed in snow. Before drinking E's mysterious black liquid, her mental image only showed a snowstorm with nothing but white as far as the eye could see. But now she could see through the snow. She even saw the shrine gate that was mentioned in her cultivation scrolls. She couldn't explain how her mental image had improved so much. Yukiko only saw a faint unworldly dark light highlight the shrine gate in the previous snowstorm, but since then, the light had disappeared, leaving the image of the shrine gate to only become more real with each cultivation cycle.

In the middle of her cultivation session, Yukidori, his teacher and guardian, Miss Eiko, and Mr. Fujita, the man put in charge of village security when the warriors went out for the season of war, walked in with much haste. Yukidori had in his hands a letter with the seal of urgent information on it. Yukiko knew something was wrong as soon as she saw them come in because interrupting someone while they were cultivating was the highest form of disrespect among fellow cultivators.

"Dori, what is going on?"

Yukidori handed his older sister the letter and said, "Mr. Fujita came to Miss Eiko after receiving this letter and tried to convince her of doing something behind your back." Yukidori stood behind Miss Eiko and poked his tongue out at Mr. Fujita, but Mr. Fujita didn't notice.

After reading the letter, Mr. Fujita knew that things would be difficult no matter what decision he made, so he chose the option that would protect him and his loved ones the most. That was why he went to get the most powerful person in the village, Miss Eiko, to help him without letting the holy maiden know about it. But his plan ended up backfiring, so he knew he couldn't go through with it.

Yukiko read the letter and felt her eyes turn cold as she looked at Mr. Fujita. There was a white glow in her retinas. Mr. Fujita was a peak tier-two middle-aged man, but he had never felt this small and insignificant in front of anyone before. As a water source user who focused on his source element instead of his source manifestation. As long as he was surrounded by snow or water, he was quite formidable in the same realm. But when his eyes met Yukiko's, he felt like his very blood had frozen. In his mind, Yukiko was the embodiment of Evil Frost, never using her abilities because she was too timid. But now, all he could see was a queen of ice and snow questioning him. He was too afraid of displeasing her.

"Thank you, Eiko, for bringing this to my attention and not working behind my back."

"Anything for the Miya family, young miss." Miss Eiko put her right hand above her heart and slightly bowed to Yukiko. She was also startled by the change in Yukiko's personality, but she hid it better than others.

"Please, take Dori back to finish his lessons for the day."

"Right away." Eiko took Yukidori by the hand, and they walked out as he waved goodbye to his older sister.

Alone with Yukiko, Mr. Fujita found himself more scared with each passing moment. The old Yukiko was gone. The quiet, lonely girl had been replaced by an ice queen. She didn't do anything to him. She just looked at him with eyes that could freeze the sun, but that was enough for him to lose any choice of defying her.

"I apologize for doing anything that would have displeased you, but I only acted in the best interest of the village."

At first, Yukiko felt a new sensation take over her whole body. For the first time in her life, she knew the feeling of being above the common rabble, and it was amazing. But the more she felt it, the more dangerous she realized having that mindset was. Shaking her head, she was back to normal, and Fujita could finally breathe again.

"You speak about what's best for the village, so let me hear you defend how you were going to catch my ill friend behind my back."

Though Yukiko wasn't the ice queen anymore, she saw how wielding her power gave her the results she needed. She thought back to all her interactions with E and tried to imitate his style of handling people. After their brief conversation, she sent a scared Mr. Fujita away and went back to Pride and E's hut.

Mr. Fujita scrambled toward his family's hut. Once inside, he went to the back room where his personal training room was located and went straight to the hidden compartment located behind the training dummy. Using his hands to form hand seals while gathering source energy, he unlocked the special seal that kept the compartment isolated from the rest of the world. When it was open, he reached his hand inside and pulled out a black talisman. Then, he sent his source energy into the talisman to contact his master.

As Yukiko went back to the hut where Pride and E were, things were different. Unlike before, when she went to the stairs, nothing happened. Yukiko made her way to the front door and walked in to see something unexpected. Laying down in his bed, Pride seemed unconscious while his arm and a copy of his missing arm made out of a dark substance moved above his head with the dark substance floating between his hands.

E had possessed Pride's body again and was forming the pill in a way Yukiko had never seen or heard of before. All she saw him do was hold the dark substance as it changed rapidly. Trying to understand what she is witnessing, Yukiko unconsciously moved forward. Once she got close enough, her presence broke E's concentration, and the dark substance lost control too quickly for E to keep it together.

Past the point of no return, the dark substance started to create a chain of small explosions that, if they occurred at the same time, would be comparable to a peak tier-two attack that was powerful enough to destroy a two-story home. With no time to waste, E's presence left Pride's body and opened a hole in the air that swallowed the explosion before it could detonate.

After narrowly escaping death, E's presence opened another hole in the air that sucked Yukiko back into the golden room.

Once he was settled, E asked Yukiko, "What do you want?"

Seeing that E seemed to not want to pursue the issue of interrupting him or seeing whatever she saw, Yukiko cut straight to the point. "I contacted all the clan allies that are near any of the safe locations you told me about a few days ago. Two of the clans have seen a highly equipped group of people quickly checking out the locations you told me about. I wouldn't bother you about this because, like you explained, it was just to know which route they were taking to reach the hidden village and how much time we would have. But just now, we caught word that a bounty has been placed on both Pride and Daisuke's heads. The group of people are spreading the information as they make their way. The bounty is so huge that I caught a guard trying to catch Pride in the name of protecting the village, but in actuality, it was just for himself."

E sat and pondered the new information. "Shit, things have escalated in a path I had hoped they wouldn't."

"What do you mean?"

"Our current plan is based off of the enemy either hiring a professional—so we would stall for time for as long as possible—or coming quietly themselves to not let any possibility of their organization finding out so as to not embarrass themselves. Now they have thrown a bucket full of meat between predators. All they have to do is sit back and watch everyone fight. Once we are too tired to fight back, they can just swoop in for the kill."

Yukiko didn't know what do. With just one move, she felt as if she was against every clan, village, or criminal in the wastelands. "What should we do?"

E pinched the bridge of his nose with his thumb and index finger while closing his eyes. Pride had been unconscious the entire time, and E had tried to ruin any chance of Pride and Daisuke staying together by telling Daisuke that Pride already planned to abandon Daisuke. But that couldn't be farther from the truth. Pride wanted to travel the world with Daisuke, the only person he considered a brother, to find out who he was and where he came from. With things having changed, E knew he couldn't risk Daisuke's safety. Otherwise, Pride might get rid of E in anger for letting something happen to his brother.

E opened his eyes. "Yukiko, you will have to make a tough decision in the following days to come. Prepare yourself because you might have to give up everything."

"What do you mean 'give up everything?'"

"The original plan was to let Pride be seen near multiple villages so that they wouldn't be able figure out where he was or where he was going. Then, after some time, he would come back and destroy the City of Noel. But now, we have to make some bold decisions. Do not disturb me for the next few days." Like usual, after E got done with saying what he wanted to say, he told Yukiko to leave, causing her to be left in more emotional turmoil.

*****

Hundreds of miles away in a secluded forest known as the Dark Woods, where no sentient being dared to approach, tall looming trees threatened to blot out the sun while there was a dense fog that blanketed the area around and inside the forest. If anyone was dumb enough to even look in its direction for a split second, that being would swear they saw something staring back. And when they turned their heads back, there was no evidence of what they thought they saw. The smart ones would realize that something wasn't right and ran away as far as possible, but the stupid ones would step into the forest and never be heard of or seen again.

Rumors had spread to anyone with ears within traveling distance that witnesses, over the last few years, had seen people running, climbing, and swinging through trees from a distance ever so briefly. Every group had their own theory that no one took seriously. There was the theory of a pack of rare hybrids having taken over the forest. Another theory was that the ghosts of all the people who died inside the forest were still haunting their resting place. The most unthinkable theory was that the forest was a safe place for runaway slaves to not be caught.

Daisuke had led dozens of runaway slaves through the only safe and easy path into the heart of the forest for years. At first, he was the only one leading others to the forest, but those inspired by him and others who wanted to be powerful later learned his way of body cultivation. At least twenty people in tier-two began to model themselves after him. With that, they developed the ability to hunt and gather, train their bodies, and rescue runaway slaves who found their way to the forest.

This morning, the leaders and their vice-captains of each respective groups sat down with Daisuke, who had been back with them for almost two weeks, and reviewed how preparations to confront the City of Noel were going. Every morning, Daisuke had this same meeting after learning from his mistake when he put Yukiko's entire village in harm's way.

"These are the points that we will focus on moving forward now that the primary and secondary defensive lines have been reinforced. With them having a map showing how to take the safe path, we have lost our hiding spot, but we know where they will come from. We can set up ambushes the deeper they make their way into the woods."

Daisuke and his people spent an hour going over different strategies and worst-case situations until someone said, "After going over everything they could throw at us, why haven't we ever thought of running?"

While a few of the younger men and women had the same question, the older and more experienced members of the group just shook their heads.

"Where would we go?" asked Daisuke. "Back to our homes, of course."

"First of all, how would we get there when we can't access any of the teleportation tunnels? Second, what about the people and families who don't have anywhere besides the City of Noel to call home?"

When the ones in favor of running away heard this, they realized they had been backed into a corner but hadn't realized it yet. Everyone else was already aware of their situation. Daisuke saw the worry on their faces and made a move. He ripped his shirt in half and pointed his thumb to his chest. On his chest was the symbol of The Merchant's slave brand. When everyone saw it, the fire in their eyes and hearts was set ablaze. Everyone used their thumb to point at their own slave branding and stood firm.

"Never forget what they took from us. Always remember why we still fight."

For too many unfortunate souls there, the rage they felt was the only thing they had to their names. For the lucky few, they still had family members, friends, and lovers believing them to have died some time ago still in the city. Even at this point, Daisuke didn't know what happened to the slaves in the City of Noel.

Chapter Thirteen

Awaken

In a large underground cave in the middle layer of the State of Moon's wasteland, there was a group of heavily equipped men and women. Wearing white martial arts robes and masks to hide their appearance were Gil Eanes's squad of trackers. Like most overseers, he had his own specialty. He spent ninety percent of his year scouting locations for his partner overseer who dealt with attacking hidden or heavily fortified locations like sects, clans, or villages. While they constantly checked the caves that were marked on the map for any signs of use or traps, the other group couldn't be any more different.

The second group was led by Robert, consisting of only his personally trained body cultivation slaves. Unlike the regular slave seal, the one that he used on them messed with their minds so that there were two voices in their heads making decisions. As more time passed, the foreign voice only got stronger, while the original voice tried to yell over the foreign voice until the original voice eventually became silenced.

While the slaves were still covered up by their hoods and cloaks, they had no protection over their bodies besides their body cultivation aura of protection. This was the very same technique Daisuke always used to keep the cold out of Pride's body and hold together all of Pride's internal organs, muscles, and bones from getting worse as he carried him to the Winter Herb Village.

Robert sat staring at the blizzard taking place outside, contemplating what was going on. The Merchant's exact orders where to scout out and quietly verify the route leading to the slaves' hidden village. Right before Robert left to carry out the orders, his father stopped him. While alone, Rod handed his son a small wooden box with a peak tier-two source lock on it and commanded him to bring back Weakness's dead body intact by wearing what was in the box when he got to the village.

Never in his life had Robert ever seen such a fervent look in his father's eyes before. All he could imagine was the purple glow that escaped his father's eyes for a moment and drew his mind. Never in his entire life had his father ever told him to defy an order from The Merchant. Robert hated everything about what his father wanted him to do. Treating a slave like an equal went against everything he had believed his whole life. But if he dared to underestimate the escaped slaves after he saw what Pride could do, he worried that he would end up dead.

After finishing his search of the area, Gil Eanes approached Robert. "We've searched this place just like all the other safe spots and found nothing again."

Robert couldn't figure out why Gil Eanes had gone along with his father's plan to spread Daisuke and Pride's descriptions and bounty, but since he treated it as if it was normal, he saw no reason to bring attention to it.

"This is the last safe location on the map before the village. Do you think nothing has happened so far because they want us to let our guards down at a careless moment?" asked Robert.

Gil Eanes shook his head. "Robert, even though those slaves may be more powerful than you first realized, you can't let the fear of the unknown blind you enough to overestimate them. While we can't explain how they got a peak tie-two body cultivation formula, it doesn't change the hard facts that they have no allies, limited resources, and no back-up plan once they become surrounded. While it is troubling to know next to nothing about that slave Weakness, how much could one slave do against a powerful group?"

The more Robert heard, the more he believed in Lü Zhi's analysis of Weakness's abilities when she had said he only seemed like he was untouchable and able to just appear and kill people out of nowhere. Robert recalled her saying that the only guards who died were ones who didn't wear tier-two armor or were too scared to activate it. Lü Zhi told him that even The Merchant only got injured because his guard was completely down. If not for that, his tier-three silk armor would have activated when his consciousness perceived imminent danger. Once his defenses were up, Weakness didn't attempt to attack him again.

After finally recalling and fully digesting Lü Zhi's analysis, Robert finally saw everything instead of the shadows of his own fears. He was calmer, letting all his worries wash away. He stood up, turned to Gil, and said, "I'm ready to move, so everyone hop back on top of those slaves' backs. Let's move forward with the bait plan. Here's to hoping the other slaves care more about their own than Daisuke and Pride."

A few days later, Daisuke was cultivating near the guard post at the first defensive line when he heard the sound of strong steps in the snow rushing toward the safe route into the forest. He steeled his resolve and was grateful that E's predictions had been spot on so far with the City of Noel sending a scouting party instead of an army first. He filled his lungs with air and source energy, then roared like a huge beast. His roar was so loud that those in the heart of the forest could hear it. Everyone knew it was time. With haste, everyone rushed to take their positions while Daisuke stood out in the open and waited for his enemies to get closer to him.

Once Robert went into the forest, he was shocked by how much warmer it was in the forest.

Then, he heard a roar. Instead of fearing the coming battle, Robert was excited for his first real battle. He summoned his halberd, and the wind surrounded his blade. Source strength coursed through his whole body, and he raised his halberd over his head as he charged forward while running at full speed.

After a few moments, Robert saw Daisuke, the slave who had made him feel inferior for so long, just standing in the middle of the hidden path like an immortal abandoned in this cruel world. Robert's words rang out. "Four and Five restrain him so we can find out where Weakness is."

Daisuke wasn't expecting to see Robert again so soon, but he got into his battle stance. He froze when he saw a glittering light come from the necklace Robert was wearing. At that moment, he felt his consciousness slip away, finding himself lost back in the memory of the day he almost lost his very mind and died. He relived his years as a slave like they were yesterday but with more intensity. The images began to speed up so quickly that his mind couldn't process the pain fast enough. A blaring noise blasted in his eardrums. With each cycle of torture, he started to focus only on the most painful memories. Then, he thought about Min's betrayal and the loss of his family until everything went red.

Gil Eanes was trailing Robert, so he would be useful for a sneak attack against any unforeseen situations. But right off the bat, things turned dangerous quickly. When Gil Eanes saw Daisuke, he felt physical pressure on the back of his scalp. He had only felt this against demonic beasts or monsters on a battlefield. Everyone, except Gil Eanes, within range of Daisuke's fury felt it, and they all stopped in their tracks. Even Gil Eanes's people who were making their way toward the second line of defense without being seen or heard stopped.

Gil Eanes finally knew that he had underestimated Daisuke, so he moved first and activated his spiritual manifestation, covering himself with source energy. Next, there was a giant nine-foot-tall white Iberian lynx that had overlapped with Gil Eanes, who could no longer be seen because he merged into his family's spiritual beast manifestation. He activated his clan's speed type technique Paws Prints in the Snow and charged forward with all his might by channeling his snow element into his paws to create multiple snow prints in the air. Creating footholds, he grabbed Robert in his mouth by the collar of his armor.

By the very skin of their teeth, the two missed the explosion that appeared right where Robert was a moment before, while the shrouded body cultivation slaves were thrown in several directions. The closest of them got hit with stray fire, causing their cloaks to burn away.

Standing in the crater, Daisuke passively generated spiritual fire in large quantities. His clothes blew in the air like he was in the middle of a storm. He looked like a sun god who had descended to battle.

Gil was terrified, not by the spiritual fire, but by what it meant. Daisuke, a slave who had never used spiritual source energy due to being branded with the bloodline destruction seal, had just used spiritual source energy. Even Daisuke, in his enraged and madden state, didn't realize that his seal had burned away. All he wanted was to destroy his enemies. A tiny voice in his head told him to burn everything. Daisuke was so blinded by his anger that he looked at the nearest assailant and raised his hand above to concentrate his new form of source energy to create a primary low tier-three fireball. The body cultivator slave called Four, while she didn't have free will due to the mind seal, was able to use the orders she had been given to save her friends while looking at Daisuke with hope that he could save them or end their suffering.

As he charged forward, Five ran headfirst into Daisuke to get him off his feet, but it felt like trying to move a large boulder. Meanwhile Four came from behind with a flying kick to Daisuke's back but had the same results. Luckily, this gave enough time for the others to get up and get some distance. However, that didn't save his attackers from retaliation. Instead of firing the fireball, Daisuke simply absorbed it into his body, catching on fire and burning Four's foot and Five's right shoulder and face. This move sent everything around him away, including his attackers.

Gil Eanes looked at the scene and became scared. No spirit techniques were used by Daisuke, but he was already on par with the fourth strongest overseer. Gil Eanes released his form, returning back to normal, and pulled out a black talisman. He channeled his source energy into it and began speaking. "All members retreat immediately. We are using the bait strategy to escape."

After that, Gil Eanes turned to Robert, steeled his resolve, and told him, "Lead my group back to the city and tell The Merchant everything we saw. Go with our plan for traveling back to leak their location to every clan or group you pass."

"Why can't you do it?" Robert asked. He was still shaking after his first brush with death.

"I have seen those eyes and that rage on the battlefield before. Daisuke is in the slave blood madness."

"What's that?"

"It is a technique of the slaver's union to control powerful slaves. Usually the madness makes them defenseless, but there are a few slaves who end up becoming raving mad and are the berserkers of slaves."

"Then we need to run. Let him kill those slaves while we go."

"That won't work. He has already burned the clothes off those slaves, so if he could, he would have been able to recognize his old friends. If I wait for him to kill one of them and he eventually figures it out, he will chase us down before we can get back just to avenge the grief he may feel. I need to get his allies to try to save them so I can pit them against each other. I have no more time. Go!"

Gil Eanes manifested his spirit again and shape-shifted back to his nine-foot human form. He charged in and activated Paws in the Snow again, saving the lives of the partially burned slaves by controlling the footholds to carry the ones he passed.

Daisuke constantly paused in between his movements, like he was struggling to control his body. Suddenly, like a blur, a white figure dragged all the "bait" deeper into the forest along the hidden trail. Seeing his prey get away, Daisuke roared like a beast, breathing fire in the air and dashing after them. He looked like someone shot a fireball after them.

Floating in an ocean-sized dark liquid all alone was one young man. With nothing in sight, all he could do to generate energy was to focus his mind to move as much of the liquid as he could, which wasn't very much. He had been in this location since he had fallen unconscious weeks ago. Unable to tell how much time was passing, he continued what he was doing to keep his mind active without wasting the energy he was generating. Usually, he used his mind and body to control and generate energy, but without access to his own body, he was stuck.

Without warning, he saw a thin red line come out of the darkness surrounding him and the ocean he was in. It dove directly into the ocean of liquid and created a path that was speeding toward him.

What is this? he thought. He told himself to not waste energy speaking without showing any signs of worry. As soon as the path reached him, the thread-like line went directly to where the slave brand was above his heart. "WHAT!" was the only thing he was able to say before his entire being caught on fire.

About Author

Oghosasere U-Edosomwan is a writer, artist, and cultural influencer committed to creating a positive representation and showcasing the many beautiful influencers of African culture. Even as a young man, his love for anime and how visual storytelling captivated so many audiences worldwide, he's been committed to painting, drawing, and writing stories that impacted people worldwide. For most of his life, Oghosasere saw how the American school system painted a degraded picture of black history rather than the parts that were rich and colorful. Once as a child his school told him he couldn't wear native attire to school even though they said to wear what he would wear to church to school for special days.

Rather than showcasing the contributions of his heritage, he noticed a lack of positive representation and stories that displayed power that he could be proud of as a young African man. Rather than highlight the problems, Oghosasere is committed to creating solutions through literary work and design elements that show people of color who love anime that there is a story that dives into their own culture's heritage. To find out more information about Oghosasere U-Edosomwan, email riseofblacksky@gmail.com.

www.ingramcontent.com/pod-product-compliance
Lightning Source LLC
Chambersburg PA
CBHW061523050726
47503CB00015B/2683